# CALL OF THE STAR DRAGON

AN EARTH FORCE SKY PATROL FILE: SOLAR YEAR 2388

## BLAZE WARD

KNOTTED ROAD PRESS

**Call of the Star Dragon**
**An Earth Force Sky Patrol File: Solar Year 2388**
Blaze Ward
Copyright © 2019 Blaze Ward
All rights reserved
Published by Knotted Road Press
www.KnottedRoadPress.com

ISBN: 978-1-64470-053-2

Cover art:
ID 7376777 © diversepixel | DepositPhoto.com

Cover and interior design copyright © 2019 Knotted Road Press

**Never miss a release!**
If you'd like to be notified of new releases, sign up for my newsletter.

I will never spam you, or use your email for nefarious purposes. You can also unsubscribe at any time.

http://www.blazeward.com/newsletter/

ALSO BY BLAZE WARD

**The Jessica Keller Chronicles**

*Auberon*

*Queen of the Pirates*

*Last of the Immortals*

*Goddess of War*

*Flight of the Blackbird*

*The Red Admiral*

*St. Legier*

*Winterhome*

**CS-405**

*Queen Anne's Revenge*

*Packmule*

*Persephone*

**Additional Alexandria Station Stories**

*The Story Road*

*Siren*

*Two Bottles of Wine with a War God*

**The Science Officer Series**

*The Science Officer*

*The Mind Field*

*The Gilded Cage*

*The Pleasure Dome*

*The Doomsday Vault*

*The Last Flagship*

*The Hammerfield Gambit*

*The Hammerfield Payoff*

**Earth Force Sky Patrol**

*Birth of the Star Dragon*

*Flight of the Star Dragon*

*Call of the Star Dragon*

*Shadow of the Star Dragon*

*Trial of the Star Dragon*

**Other Science Fiction Stories**

*Myrmidons*

*Moonshot*

*Menelaus*

*Earthquake Gun*

*Moscow Gold*

*Fairchild*

*White Crane*

***The Collective* Universe**

*The Shipwrecked Mermaid*

*Imposters*

GUILTY

GARETH SUPPRESSED a heavy sigh when the Bailiff paused, turned the page he was reading, and looked up at the judge, defendants, and court room.

"Last page," the man promised wearily. He stopped and took a long drink of water from a glass sitting on the counter in front of him.

The rest of the room seemed to relax as well. It had been nearly three hours, just reading all the charges publicly for the first time. As public as this room was, anyways.

"And finally, the defendants are accused of four counts of High Treason," the bailiff continued. "And one count of Attempting to Overthrow the *Accord of Souls* By Illegal Force."

Gareth grinned as the man picked up the enormous stack of papers, tapped them into a clean pile, and walked across the court room to rest them on the bench in front of the presiding judge.

That worthy rested a weary hand on the pile, nearly an inch think, and scowled at the defendants seated in front of him at a low table, the Yuudixtl scientist criminals: Morty and Xiomber.

The judge was an older woman, Gareth would have guessed. Perhaps his Mom's age, with all the wear and lines of a hard, disciplined life.

Not a woman to trifle with, even today. Again, like Mom.

He wondered how well she could bake an apple pie.

"How do the defendants plead?" she asked it a fatigued voice.

They had been at it all morning, and it was almost lunch time.

Morty turned to the attorney representing them with a confused look. That man was rather exhausted as well, but holding up well.

"That's only six hundred and twenty-seven charges," Morty said quietly.

The room was still so silent that the words carried.

"The State skipped all the jaywalking, speeding tickets, overdue books, and parking violations you two listed," he muttered back.

"Oh," Morty chirped. "Gotcha."

Gareth watched Morty, dressed in an orange prison jumpsuit, push his chair back, stand with great ceremony and solemnity, in spite of being hand-cuffed, and grin at the judge. Next to him, Xiomber did the same, perhaps a little slower. Maybe he had been napping.

Gareth would have liked to see the smiles on the two Yuudixtls faces, but he was back in the galley, several rows behind the two scientists, so he had to settle for listening to their voices instead. He could imagine it, though, just from the gleeful tones.

"Guilty, Your Honor," Morty called cheerfully.

"Also guilty, Your Honor," Xiomber joined his egg-brother a moment later.

The Judge, for all her seriousness, seemed nonplussed.

"You understand, gentlemen, that you intend to plead guilty to the only two crimes in my statute book that carry the possibility of capital punishment?" she asked slowly, waiting patiently for the two goofballs to suddenly realize what they had said.

"I do, Your Honor," Xiomber said, maybe morosely. Maybe it was just tiredness.

Gareth felt the need for coffee, and he'd been able to slightly doze over the last few hours. Talyarkinash, sitting beside him, had nudged him in the ribs a few times when he had started snoring.

"You betcha, Lady," Morty said.

For the briefest moment, Gareth wondered if the woman judge was going to lean forward and fling her gavel across the court room like a throwing knife, to bash Morty square in the forehead like a bolt from Zeus.

She looked capable of it.

But after a moment, she reconsidered.

"In light of other circumstance, and requests from the Prosecution, the defendants are hereby found Guilty of all charges and remanded to State Custody, pending a sentencing hearing currently unscheduled," she said evenly, bashing that gavel onto her desk top instead. "This Court is dismissed."

The entire room rose as one. Talyarkinash was

obviously expecting it as much as Gareth, so she didn't miss a beat.

After all, she was the only other person in here besides Morty and Xiomber who weren't wearing the uniform of the Constabulary. Blue-gray bodysuits and tunics, for the most part, although a few of the more senior officers and officials present were in really fancy attire. Even the judge under her black robes.

Two Constabulary Explorers, the equivalent of Deputy Agents that Gareth would have seen were he back home in an Earth Force Sky Patrol courtroom, led the two convicted criminals off to wherever they were going to be fed lunch.

Gareth watched Senior Constable Jackeith Grodray and Constable Eveth Baker turn and approach from the front row, surrounded by other men and women departing. Several paused long enough to offer congratulations and such to the two officers, which they took good-naturedly.

Grodray was a serious cop. Intellectual and stern, but affable for the most part. As a Vanir, the man was seven foot three, but rather lanky and skinny, coming in at barely three hundred pounds.

Since he had been transformed from human to Vanir, Gareth now had an inch of height on the other man, but at least forty pounds of bulk, mostly muscle.

But Grodray was also a cypher. He appeared as a Senior Constable in public, a Level-4. A simple detective, back home. But in reality he was a Prime Inspector, a Level-7. A free agent with authority to pursue any crime, anywhere, and expect the willing assistance of every cop and civilian he encountered along the way.

Eveth Baker was smaller than Grodray, but still big for a Vanir woman. Six foot seven and two hundred and forty pounds of grit, muscle, and tough rolled up in an athletic brunette body. Not that Gareth would ever consider her more than a cop.

He had Pippa to think about. Back home, waiting for him. Pippa unknowing that he was even alive, and that he could never return to Earth. Even if he somehow did manage it, he would be a monster.

That he wasn't even human anymore.

He had been modified. Talyarkinash, Morty, and Xiomber, the only three civilians present in the courtroom today, had reprogrammed his DNA to make him a Vanir. Bigger, stronger, faster, and smarter than ninety-nine percent of even that impressive species.

And then they had gone beyond that, even if it had been at his insistence. They had tapped into something Talyarkinash called his *latent psionic potential* to let the former human Gareth trigger a transformation into a twenty-seven-meters-long flying lizard form that could breathe fire.

A Star Dragon.

It had been the only thing Gareth could think of at the time to make him dangerous enough to take on Marc Sarzynski. *Maximus.* Another human, the only other human in the *Accord of Souls*, Gareth hoped. The man vying to become the overlord of the underworld. The Master of Crime.

And a man who, at one time would have been Gareth's Best Man, on the day he finally wed Pippa.

Maybe it was just as well that such a day was never coming now.

Grodray came to a halt before Gareth, looking slightly up at him with a stern glare.

"That's done," he announced so quietly that perhaps only the two of them and the two females close by heard. "Now the next part. Come with me."

Gareth waited for Grodray and Baker to pass, and then nodded Talyarkinash to precede him. They were the last four out of the court room, a sanctuary of law in the midst of a semi-secret, Constabulary research facility on *Irron*.

Gareth had been brought here so the Constables could study the genetic engineering Talyarkinash had programmed into him.

Every other one of the seventeen species in the *Accord of Souls* had been fixed by the Chaa, the Elders, fifty thousand years ago. Sixteen of the those species had been uplifted into their current forms at the time, and most of the Vanir had been reduced to a rough equivalence. The few remaining Chaa had then transformed themselves into gods of some sort and gone looking for the One True God who had created everything.

Nobody had expected humans to suddenly become a technological species in that time, so the Chaa had left them alone.

Which was a dreadful mistake on their part. The rest of the *Accord* was stuck in their forms and could not be modified in any significant way, beyond fixing flaws and changing hair and skin color.

Nobody but Gareth could become a Star Dragon.

Except, perhaps, another human.

# ALTERNATIVES

MARC SMILED as he considered the machine in front of him. It was off right now, but that was purely a safety measure.

On, it could be lethal.

Standing next to him in the small lab workshop was Zorge, an older Nari scientist turned spymaster who was still with Marc after so many of the others had fled or been captured.

"What am I looking at?" the Nari asked as Marc touched at the machine.

It was manlike in silhouette. Around six feet tall. Bipedal. Two arms ending in human-like hands with opposable thumbs.

"My kind called this an android," Marc purred.

Zorge only slightly flinched at the implications.

Humans were considered so dangerous that all knowledge of the *Accord of Souls* was blocked. There was a whole astronomy division dedicated to making sure that no signals from any *Accord* planet ever made it to Earth to be picked up and possibly give those xenocidal maniacs any clue that they weren't alone in the universe.

Marc had been human, once. Had been kidnapped via wormhole and brought here by a crime lord who wanted his own personal killer. Before that man realized he couldn't control such a beast.

So Marc took over. But Zorge stayed.

"Android," the Nari man mused, his ears flickering back and forth in a rhythm with his whiskers. "What do you do with it?"

"At one time, it was considered a labor-saving device," Marc replied. "You could program it to do things instead of humans having to. All the boring and mundane, or the very dangerous. Androids fell out of fashion a long time ago and never got used in any numbers."

"Why not?" Zorge asked. "Sounds like a useful thing, to be able to just tell a machine to clean the floors, or rush into a burning building to rescue people."

"Oh, humans still have *robots*," Marc stressed the difference. "But those are automated systems that are engineered and optimized for to do one thing only. Like a small disk about a foot across and six inches tall that has a brush and a vacuum built in, to automatically sweep the rugs on a daily schedule. Or mighty factory robots that pick up three pieces of a vehicle, drop them into perfect alignment, and weld them exactly true every time. Androids are generalists."

"Okay," Zorge reached up with one paw and scratched at his muttonchop sideburns absently. "So why are we needing one?"

"Androids can be programmed to do a few, repetitive tasks that lets them replace human workers. Or Nari, or Grace. Whoever," Marc smiled. "And they will be obedient to me, because they have been programmed that way."

Marc saw the lightbulb come on in Zorge's eyes. The old Nari liked to pretend to be a simple scientist who dabbled as a spymaster from time to time, but Marc knew the truth. Knew how many citizens of the *Accord* had met an untimely end at the hands of the Nari man.

Even Maiair and Yooyar, his Warreth cohorts that, with Zorge, formed his inner council, had only killed half as many people as the Nari had in his rise within the crime organization.

"They won't rat you out to the Constables," Zorge breathed heavily. "And they'll carry guns, but they aren't bound by the *Accord*, unless you program them thus."

"Exactly," Marc's grin turned feral.

"So what about the rest of us?" Zorge asked carefully.

Marc turned more fully to watch the scientist. It was important that his inner circle stay loyal. They were the basis of building his new empire.

"These do one thing," Marc explained carefully. "They will kill things. That's all. They don't talk to people. Don't build. Don't do anything else except protect me, us, from Constables and other criminals."

"Do they have to kill?" Zorge asked, obviously uncomfortable, in spite of his own background.

Very few members of the *Accord* were born broken enough that killing didn't do something bad and strange in their heads. People like Zorge had managed to overcome it, usually in rage or fear. Flight or fight syndrome.

"It has a hand," Marc said. "What you put in that hand is your choice. These things are tools, just like hammers or guns. We will retain control. But I am never going to put my safety in the hands of someone I don't trust again. That comes down to you and the girls. Nobody else. When we rebuild the organization, maybe there will be others."

"Understood, boss," Zorge nodded. And then he paused for a moment.

Marc watched the furry scientist walk slowly around the machine again, studying it from all angles before he stopped and looked at Marc.

""Does it have to be this size?" Zorge asked, his whole face screwed a little sideways in concentration. It was almost of a height with the Nari.

"As opposed to?" Marc asked, intrigued.

He had expected a major argument with the man. After all, killer robots on the loose was almost as bad a threat as humans. Like he had been.

But something about the machine had piqued the scientist in the Nari, obviously.

"Two thoughts," Zorge answered distantly. "One, why not make one nine or ten feet tall, to scare the hell out of even the Vanir? Or maybe fifteen feet tall? Something huge."

Marc paused and considered. He had been thinking in human terms again. Six feet tall, as a labor-saving robot soldier who wouldn't discretely call the cops and narc on him when he slept.

But Vanir males were often over seven feet tall. He himself was seven foot four, these days, as was Gareth. Maybe he did need something that could overawe even *Those Left Behind*, the Vanir who liked to think of themselves as the direct descendants of the Chaa, in a galaxy where everyone else had been uplifted?

"I'll consider it," Marc said, listening to both the angel on his left shoulder as well as the devil on the right. "Two?"

"Two," Zorge replied grimly. "Do we need one big enough to wrestle with a Star Dragon?"

# SEEKER

ROYSTON LOUGHTY, PhD, WMU, FRS, CBE, CStJ, considered the massive, complicated device resting on his lab bench like a beached whale. He was the man affectionately known on this station as "The Big Brain" but even he was half-certain that much of what was resting in front of him could be just as adequately explained as magic as it could physics.

But he was a scientist. Doctor of Physics. Warden of the Mathematical Union. Fellow of the Royal Society. Commander, British Empire. Commander, Order of St. John. One of the preeminent physicists in the solar system, and certainly the top expert on the types of solar radiation that Earth Force employed.

Only a handful of men, and one woman, could even follow the details of the paper he had written. Dr. Sir Westfield van Duren-Abbott PhD, FRS, GMU, KCB, GBE was one of them. The Grand Old Man of science himself.

Royston expected that one of the two of them would eventually have to write a second paper, just to boil it all down into terms that the average genius mathematician or physicist could follow, to say nothing of the man on the street.

Magic, indeed.

The door to his vast lab opened as he pulled a pipe from the pocket of his tweed jacket and considered stuffing it into his mouth. Something to chew on, to keep him from grinding his teeth in frustration.

"So it must be going well," Philippa Loughty, his only daughter, smiled and laughed as he walked in and spied him. "You only smoke that damnable pipe when you think you've hit a dead end and haven't yet convinced yourself you've solved whatever problem confronted you."

"Eh?" he looked up, surprised and perhaps abashed.

She might be right. Pippa usually was. That was why he had taken her on as his assistant, when all the major universities refused to admit a woman into their PhD programs in higher math or astrophysics. Nobody else was willing to admit that a woman might be the intellectual equal of a man.

Fools.

Pippa walked close and kissed him on the cheek. She was a bright spot of color in her uniform as an Women's Auxiliary of Earth Force Sky Patrol. Crimson skirt just past her knees. Matching tunic as long as a blazer, double-breasted over the left with gold buttons and gold embroidery lacing. A yellow stripe edged the tunic and the collar, making her look like a true professional woman, emphasizing the red hair and bright green eyes of her Scots heritage.

"Is it done?" she asked, spreading a hand to indicate the machine on the desk.

Royston put the pipe back in his pocket, aware that he just might bite through the stem in frustration.

"Theoretically," he announced in an irritated growl. "The gentlemen who built it to my specifications and designs had to do some fancy work inside in places, and could not actually test it."

"Why not, Father?" Pippa's beautiful face scrunched up in confusion.

"Well, for one, the power requirements would require at least eighteen percent of the full output of this station's power plant, dear," Royston replied. "I have not yet gotten approval to set up such an experiment, even to try to configure the machine. Plus there is the safety aspect."

"Safety?" she asked. "How dangerous could it be?"

"We'll be opening a wormhole in physical space, Pippa," Royston scowled at her. "It might suddenly turn into a black hole and destroy this entire station. If we were on the ground, it might destroy the Earth."

She grinned and kissed him on the cheek again, lacing her arm through his elbow.

"And Oppenheimer had the exact same concerns at Alamogordo, Father," she reminded him. "At a standard deviation in the same rough neighborhood as a cash register spontaneously turning into an ice cream machine. Certainly, if it requires that much power to simply open, it won't have enough to trigger any sort of feedback loop faster than you could cut the feeds, could it?"

She reached out a hand and tapped the one device he had insisted be external to everything else. A guillotine large enough to kill a rabbit perhaps, poised on powerful springs to sever the immense power cables that would feed the ravenous beast when he activated it.

Without enough power, the theory said that the wormholes would collapse back into Einstinian physics immediately, leaving only a trace of radiation. That trace that had first set him on this mad quest six months ago.

Even in his own mind, it sounded like the worst mixture of a lurid spy thriller combined with the silliest, most over-the-top scientifictional tale.

Open a wormhole in space. Reach through and kidnap a man from his own cabin, never to be seen again.

To what end?

And yet, six months ago, Gareth St. John Dankworth, Field Agent of Earth Forces Sky Patrol, had vanished. Gone. Leaving no trace at all, except a detectable type of radiation that had no place in the current Extended Model of Physics. The understanding of the universe accepted by everyone else.

In pursuing that, Pippa had accused him of having an incomplete understanding of physics and the universe. Which had galled him all the more, when he realized that she had been right. So he invented more physics, more mathematics.

And built himself a machine. One that frightened him as much as he thrilled at the possibilities. Could they really travel through wormholes to other worlds? Explore the universe?

What would they find out there?

But, more importantly, *who* would they find?

It had not been a natural occurrence, when Gareth vanished. Someone had opened that tube, Royston was sure.

Why? And why Gareth?

"Father?" Pippa broke into his train of thought.

"Hmm?"

"Is this device safe enough to test?" she asked, voice suddenly a bit more abashed.

"Indeed, Pippa," Royston tried to assuage her. "The cut-out will function perfectly, severing the line with non-conductive blades that are irresistible. I have considered a dead-man switch as well, so that if something were to happen and I lost control, loosening my grip would trigger the blades as well."

"So why then are you so frustrated?" Pippa stayed close, leaned against him.

With her mother gone, it was just the two of them. Had been for nearly two decades. And she was as brilliant, and as stubborn as her mother had been.

"I think it will work," Royston mumbled nervously.

"And?"

"What if we are not alone in the universe, dear child?" Royston asked.

# TROUBLE

GARETH FOLLOWED the other three into a small conference room that had been set up for lunch, glasses and linens already laid out. Stewards were just placing plates of hot food and filling glasses, and they quickly departed.

Must have been following the trial and just waiting for everyone to get out.

Quickly, they sat, three Vanir at a table full-sized for them and a Nari whose chair and foot rest had been elevated until she was comfortable enough to eat with the others.

Lunch wasn't cow, but the meat was close enough. And the vegetable wasn't a potato. Wasn't even remotely related to a potato, but it served a close enough purpose to hold butter, sour cream, and bacon. Or the gustatory equivalents thereof.

Food went quickly and they settled for coffee. Gareth was glad that none of the others smoked tobacco. That smell would just undercut a fine meal.

Grodray fixed him with a professorial eye.

"It has been five months," Grodray said in a characteristically terse tone. "People who saw you flying above *Orgoth Vortai* have largely written the entire thing off as some sort of crazy, massive public relations stunt organized as part of the *Accord* Ball. We have not worked to dissuade them of that notion."

Gareth nodded. He had done his duty that night, saving Morty and Xiomber and the driver of the van from dying when the crime boss Omerlon shot out the controls of the flying machine. That had gotten the man convicted of attempted murder of a Constabulary officer, so he was going to rot in prison forever.

But they had also laid low in the time since.

Partly, that was Grodray and Baker suddenly breaking open one of the biggest corruption scandals in the history of the *Accord of Souls*. They had been too busy chasing and catching all the cockroaches revealed when someone turned the kitchen light on.

Gareth had returned to *Irron* with Talyarkinash to train and study his abilities more, and eventually Morty and Xiomber joined them, to try to understand what a Star Dragon was, and what it could and couldn't do. The boys were now permanent convicts, but that really didn't mean anything, as far as Gareth could tell.

"Now that things have calmed down, the decision has been made to put you back out in the field," Grodray continued. "Maximus has vanished completely this time, and nobody is even talking about the man. We can't tell if that's good news or bad, but all leads have dried up in the time we spent dismantling Omerlon's organization. And dealing with a number of bent or criminal officers of the courts that needed to be removed as well. Baker?"

Every eye turned to Grodray's partner now. Eveth Baker would be a Prime Investigator soon. Of that Gareth had no doubts. She was young, barely four years older than Gareth, but she was being groomed for big things.

Like running Gareth in the field. Possibly being the senior officer to him, if Gareth was made a full-fledged officer in the future, rather than just… whatever he was now. Trying to do the right thing as best he knew how.

She took a deep breath and seemed to transform herself away from the ball of angry energy she usually presented, to something calm and almost scholarly.

"Gareth, I went back and read your report about the *Accord* Ball," Baker said simply, eyes locking with him across the table. "Before you spotted Morty and Xiomber, you were in the process of establishing a very useful contact with Diệu Ahn Jamart, an extremely wealthy art collector."

Gareth blushed as he thought back to the night. Her outfit that night had barely covered her enough for polite company, even in that crowd, showing off an extraordinary amount of pinkish, tanned skin marked all over with large freckle patterns, from the bits he had been able to see. And imagine. It had been like standing next to a bipedal giraffe.

"That's right," Gareth said. "I have not contacted her as yet, pending orders. I am not sure I would be able to."

"The number she gave you was her personal

comm," Baker said with a smug smile. "We've confirmed with the right people that it still works."

Gareth felt all the blood drain out of his entire body, rushing instead into his face. That night, he had been moments from being pulled by the incredibly tall Borren woman into an interspecies erotica exhibit at the *Accord* Hall of Arts.

An interactive exhibit.

It was a Grace museum. A people who were human-sized bipeds that could pass for human at a distance. Until you got close enough to realize that instead of hair they had a mass of writing tentacles equipped with extensive sensory capabilities. And that they liked to touch.

Finding those two criminal scientists at the last moment had been the greatest breakthrough in his life, as far as he was concerned.

Gareth gulped again. Baker seemed to be enjoying his discomfort as she watched silently.

Talyarkinash wasn't any better at hiding her grin.

"Enough," Grodray growled. Dad cracking the whip.

Baker sobered immediately.

"You will contact her," Baker said. "You will continue to use the cover of a traveling art critic and reporter with no last name. One who writes under a penname. It is our hope that she will provide you access to elements of society that the Constabulary is excluded from."

The dissipated wealthy, Gareth supposed. Those people with so much money that they couldn't spend it all if they tried. The kind who collected esoteric art. The really weird stuff.

"Am I real?" Gareth scowled at Baker

"Real?" she replied, utterly confused.

"Is there actually a bi-line somewhere?" Gareth said. "Some authentic art critic and fashion reporter from the Constabulary who does write this sort of thing, when you need to send someone under cover?"

Baker paused and looked sideways at Grodray.

The older man smiled like he had just won a bet.

"Indeed there is, Gareth," Grodray said. "You'll travel to meet him shortly, and we will supply you with a collection of things you supposedly have written over the last few years, so that you can be prepared, in case someone tries to trip you up later."

"How many of me are there?" Gareth said. "No, don't answer that. Above my pay grade and I don't really want to know.

Grodray just smiled.

"At present, we do not have any leads," Baker continued. "Nor do we necessarily expect anything out of such contacts, but you are to keep your eyes open. If something comes up, your job is to call me or Grodray and let us handle it. You will not get yourself into trouble, nor will you display your capabilities. Am I clear?"

"Yes, ma'am," Gareth nodded sharply. "Deep cover."

"Deep enough," Grodray spoke up now. "As your cover is a reporter, you can remain in regular contact with your editor. Baker will run you just like an editor would. You will write up reports as if they were going to be edited and reviewed before publication in some magazine, so keep your language clear, and don't be afraid to include whatever background materials you feel appropriate."

"What do we actually know about Diệu Ahn?" Gareth asked. "I read a brief bio five months ago, but nothing since."

"She divorced one enormously wealthy husband, and outlived a second one," Baker said grimly. "Somewhere in the top five hundred richest people in the *Accord*. Collects things that catch her eye. She will attempt to seduce you."

"She can try," Gareth growled under his breath.

"Understood," Baker acknowledged. "This is more a warning than an expectation of success."

Baker turned the firehose of her attention to Talyarkinash now.

"Doctor Liamssen, now that the two Yuudixtl have been officially remanded into custody, you will be transferred with them to work directly with Dr. Fitzroy, with whom you have previously consulted. Until we can capture or eliminate Marc Sarzynski, there is a significant risk that he will try to bring in more humans, as well as potentially performing experiments on himself to match Gareth."

"Okay," Talyarkinash replied evenly. "What part will I play?"

"We need the three of you to build me a human detector," Baker smiled savagely. "Gareth is supposedly Vanir now, as is Sarzynski, but the transformation does not appear to have made either of them part of the *Accord*, at least that psionic link we all share to one degree or another."

"I see," the Nari geneticist said. "And we need to find out how to identify a transformed human?"

"The four of you, with Dalton, are the principal

experts on humans I have available, Doctor," Baker replied simply. "We cannot protect the *Accord* unless we can identify infiltrators. How they are dealt with is another department, and one I'm not interested in. We're the hunters."

"Will we remain on *Irron*?" Talyarkinash asked.

"You will for now," Grodray spoke up. "Eve and I will trail Gareth at a safe enough distance, working mainly from a private office on *Orgoth Vortai*. Dalton Fitzroy is a Prime Investigator, like myself, so she will be able to punch through any bureaucratic issues that come up. Questions?"

Gareth and Talyarkinash both shook their heads. It was too early to know anything, but they had been planning for this. Now it was time to put everything into action.

Gareth just wished he had Pippa here to talk to. Diệu Ahn as likely to make unacceptable demands on him, and he would have to find a way to navigate the Scylla and Charybdis of the case.

It would not be fun.

PRISONER 1000786128

MORTY PUT the book down as the lock to his cell rattled loudly.

It was a compact space, if a bit roomy for a Yuudixtl, being Vanir-scaled. Bed permanently attached to the wall as a shelf. Sink and toilet in a corner. Small bookshelves hanging from another corner. Light switch by door that only worked to lower things to dimness, not darkness.

Learning to sleep with the lights on had been the hardest part of prison. Even the food wasn't all that bad. Of course, until today, the cops had wanted to keep him and his egg-brother cooperative.

This morning, he had sealed his fate.

Now, he got to find out what that would be.

The big cop entered as the door opened. Grodray. The terror of the underworld, according to everything Morty had known about the man, back when he was still a full-time criminal scientist.

Grodray brought a wooden chair into the room

and sat on it as Morty put his book off to one side and concentrated on the man.

The door closed loudly and the locks shot home with a thump.

Silence fell.

Vanir were huge. Seven feet tall. Twice Morty's size. Nearly three times his weight. Skin without scales, but with fur in strange places. Grodray might actually look pretty good, if he grew a beard. It had made a helluva change in Gareth.

Course, might also come in completely gray now, too. There was that. Yuudixtl just got yellower in the scales as they aged.

Expressive and communicative face, at least compared to the hard ridges and bone of a Yuudixtl. Pointy ears that looked like they should move, catlike, like Talyarkinash Liamssen's did, but didn't.

Oh well.

Not a lot of communication going on with that face right now. Maximus had been like that. Hard, cold stare designed to unnerve people. Usually worked.

Morty wasn't that impressed. He cocked his head to one side and just sort of grinned at the guy.

What more can you do to me besides sentence me to death, officer?

Silence.

"Why?" Grodray announced suddenly.

Morty cocked his head the other way.

"Could you narrow that down, Grodray?" Morty asked. "I've done some amazingly stupid shit over the years, so I'm not sure which bad decision you want to talk about today."

Pause. Hard-ass cop stare.

"So let's start with Gareth," Grodray said. "I've read all your statements and reports, Morty, so don't give me that line of crap. Tell me the truth about the man."

Morty took a deep breath. Only Xiomber knew that story, as far as those sorts of things went.

Not that he expected a cop like Grodray to get it. But what the hell? They would be recording whatever he said for posterity anyway, after he was dead.

"Because I thought I was God, the first time," Morty finally replied.

"God?" Grodray's grunt was not all that amused.

"Cinnra wanted himself a human," Morty said. "A killer. So I got him one. Well, me and Xiomber did. He's the smart one. I'm the sneaky one. Went and located the baddest, most dangerous human criminal I could find. Turned out he was a renegade cop. He came, he saw, he conquered. Cinnra's dead and Marc Sarzynski takes the name Maximus. And now we're going places."

"Such as?" Grodray asked.

"If we'd done nothing to stop him, Maximus would have taken over the entire underworld on *Zathus* once and for all by now," Morty said. "Then the government itself. Because nothing could have stopped him. Nothing at all, okay?"

"Okay," Grodray allowed.

I mean, if we're going to be honest here, cop, let's talk turkey.

"But then I woke up one morning and my house was on fire," Morty continued. "Just a small one, but what do you do when the stove is suddenly on fire and it's too big for you to put out alone?"

"Call for help," Grodray nodded.

"Yeah, but what kind of help?" Morty felt his face and voice get all growly now. "And it is my fault that Maximus is likely to take over the whole shooting match. If I hadn't thought I was a God, I wouldn't have built the machine to grab the guy, one step ahead of his own cops arresting him, back home. Turns out later that Gareth, of all people, had Sarzynski's gang cornered, and had caught most of them. But they missed out on the big guy."

"But—" Grodray started to say, but Morty cut him off.

"So if I burn the whole damned house down, I don't really get to complain about sleeping in the backyard when it rains, do I?" Morty snapped. "Once I woke up to that, the rest was easy. Set the psionic parameters almost exactly the opposite of what they had been before, look for a signal that matches, and realize the guy's a cop. A human cop, of all things. But he's the best fit I can find if I want to stop Maximus from taking over the whole damned galaxy. Kidnapping Gareth and bringing him to the *Accord* might be the biggest crime I've committed in a lifetime of debauchery, but let me tell you this. It was also the smartest thing I've ever done. And I'd do it again, if I had to. When we got separated from Gareth that first time, on *Hurquar*, he told us to find another Earth Force Sky Patrol Agent if we had to, and explain it all to them, using his name."

"Treason and Attempting to Overthrow the *Accord*," Grodray quoted at him, but Morty wasn't having any of it.

"That was Maximus," the Yuudixtl said angrily. "Gareth was to stop Sarzynski and save the damned *Accord*."

"And the Star Dragon?" Grodray asked.

"Kid's crazy as a junebug, Grodray," Morty replied. "We were just gonna turn him into another Vanir, so he had an even chance to hide and stop the crooks. He wanted something big and splashy. Something that would strike utter terror into the hearts and minds of criminals everywhere. If I thought I could have wings and breathe fire like that, I would have stayed in legitimate business, buddy."

"Okay," Grodray nodded. "So what do I do with you and your egg-brother?"

"I told Xiomber that I'd rather spend forty years complaining that I had read the entire prison library twice, than be dead," Morty said. "I can't imagine you trust me, whatever I do or say, so what can I do?"

"You willing to work?" Grodray asked in a hard voice. "You and your brother? To spend the rest of your lives trying to save galactic civilization?"

"Yeah," Morty said simply. "Can't talk for him, but you and Gareth are the only things protecting us from Maximus."

"I've got the entire Constabulary, Morty," Grodray growled back.

"And it won't be enough, cop," Morty snapped. "Unless you know something I don't."

"We'll see."

Grodray rose suddenly. Lifted the immense chair easily and carried it to the door. One mighty fist banged three times on the metal door and it opened.

Morty found himself alone in his cell again as the

door slammed and locked, wound all the way up to the point he hopped off the bed and began to pace.

How the hell would *he* stop Maximus, it was up to him?

# REPORTER

THE HOTEL LOBBY was vast enough to have its own telephone zone, as Gareth walked in from the busy street.

Cream and tan marble on the floor, supporting white, stone columns that dominated a three-story vaulted space with two mezzanines wrapped around the edge, with glass fronts of their own so people could see everything. There were people here, but most of them looked like they were trying to be seen, rather than actually waiting for anyone.

This hotel had that kind of reputation. Famous people passed through, staying and making their reputation as much as the hotel's. Perhaps they were here to be interviewed on their next project. It was a good place for an undercover fashion and art reporter to use as his base, while he penetrated the world of elite luxury.

Gareth had studied all the things he had supposedly written over the last few years under a pseudonymous penname. Fashion and art, for the most part, with the occasional foray into writing puff pieces on fabulous vacation spots for the extremely wealthy.

The kinds of places where your name was on a secret list, or you weren't even allowed to know it existed.

Being undercover and not being required to be dressed as a dandy, he had fallen back on a replica of the outfit he first got when he came to the *Accord of Souls*. Baker had approved the replacement for the identical outfit Gareth still kept in his closet. The one that was still only human sized. Gareth had considered adding a cowboy-style hat, but decided that would be too much, most of the time.

So comfortable cowboy boots with a heel high enough for roping, but low enough to walk considerable distances, and not too sharp a toe. Black dungaree pants, baggy enough that they covered his boots instead of tucking into them. He still missed his Sky Patrol tunic, but in its place he had a plain, white T-shirt, underneath a button-down, button-up shirt in Sky Patrol plaid colors. So he was almost home. A blue denim jacket with bronzed buttons on the breast pockets and a small SP button stuck through the flap of the left breast pocket completed the look.

The only addition of note had been a plain, gold ring on his left hand. He could lie and pretend to be engaged, and use that as an excuse to turn down invitations gracefully. Explaining the truth to someone was impossible, anyway.

So here he was. Dressed up and ready to go.

As it was, he already felt like if he added a pair of toy, nickel capguns in twin holsters, he'd be seven years old again and all set to play Cowboys and Indians.

But this outfit worked. All he had to do was wear it into Talyarkinash's lab and watch her eyes light up. Or walk up to the lunchroom and sit where the female members of the Constabulary could watch him.

He had no idea how or why, but it was apparently *a good thing*, to hear Baker and Grodray talk. And it helped keep him out of a jail cell, where he really, honestly deserved to be, all things considered.

Or a freak show.

Gareth didn't let himself go down that path.

A self-important Grace in a fancy suit accosted him as he crossed the floor, looking around. The tentacles for hair just added an edge of weird to Gareth's day.

"May I help you, sir?" he asked in a voice filled with serene, superior doubt on the topic.

Obviously, one of *those* people who had wandered into the wrong building by accident. Or not known to use the delivery entrance around back.

Something about the man's silent sneer just rubbed Gareth entirely the wrong way.

Rather than answer, Gareth drew himself up to his full height, glaring down at the man from a head and a half higher. He reached inside the comfortable jacket and pulled out an oversized card.

"Is my room ready?" Gareth snapped at the Grace in a peremptory voice.

Mother would have taken a wooden spoon to his bottom for such a tone, but she wasn't here, and the role called for it, apparently.

The difference in the Grace was night and day.

Suddenly, Gareth wasn't an imposter, but *Important People* who must be fawned over, and how could the Grace man have possibly make such a terrible mistake?

"I'm sure it is," the Grace said, carefully taking the card from his hand to inspect it before swiftly leading Gareth to the discrete desk off to one side.

A cute Nari girl, barely out of her teens but composed and professional, stood behind the counter and took the card from the man.

"Mary will take excellent care of you, sir," the concierge promised in an utterly obsequious tone. "Did you have luggage?"

"It will be delivered this afternoon," Gareth noted absently, drolly. Playing a role he barely believed himself.

Seriously, were people normally like this?

"Very good, sir," and the Grace was gone.

"Just Gareth?" Mary asked carefully. "No last name?"

"That's right," he said, playing the role Baker and Grodray had assigned him. Mysterious and aloof.

"Everything is already taken care of, then, sir," Mary said, looking down at a screen on her side of the desk.

She paused for a moment, sniffing him. He had enough experience with Talyarkinash doing the same thing to note the way the nostrils worked. And the whiskers and ears twitching out of tune with each other.

"May I escort you to your room, Gareth?" Mary asked brightly.

Gareth swallowed the snarl that wanted to blister the girl. He would just have to get used to a world where females could be just as forward as males, bizarre as it was. Where he would be absently propositioned for meaningless sexual encounters by strangers in hotel lobbies, if he wasn't careful.

Worse, once he dove into this world, they would frequently be people with money, who were unused to being rebuffed.

Tough, buddy.

"Absolutely," Gareth allowed, rocking his weight back onto his heels.

She came around the counter with a plastic keycard in one hand and a small envelope that she handed him, passing too close for politeness. Just barely brushing herself against his side.

The elevator ride was pleasant, as long as he focused on the lights and not the young girl focused on him.

The room was larger inside than Patrol Cutter *Bellerophon*, his first independent command, had been. Huge. Suite didn't do it justice, as it had a full kitchen and dining room, three subsidiary bedroom suites, and a salon large enough for his junior high chess club to hold tournaments in, plus a balcony that was four meters deep and ran the entire width of the suite, which was a significant radius of the hotel itself.

Mary had to show him everything. He smiled and thought happy thoughts until he managed to get her out the door and drop the deadbolt into place. He considered sliding a heavy chair into the way as well, but stopped himself and moved out to the balcony to relax and enjoy the view.

They were on *Morthri*, the original homeworld of the Nari. The skies weren't the blue of *Earth* that he kept expecting when he looked up. Nor the greener skies of *Irron* where he had come from most recently. But at the same time, the reddish hue overhead wasn't the cotton candy of *Orgoth Vortai*.

The Underhives of Mars were probably the closest comparison he could make, in those rare times when you got out onto the surface to walk around, rather than staying safely below ground.

Watching the sun slowly set as he stood on his balcony, he could see the inland sea in the near distance, and a swimming pool so close below that a cliff diver could have made a living.

"Well, hello," a voice came from his right. Female. Cheery. Welcoming. "It is so good to see you again."

Gareth turned at the voice and located the speaker. He watched Diệu Ahn lift her head up to smile at him, from where she had been lying face down on a lounge chair sunbathing. Hopefully, she had a towel below her, because as near as Gareth could tell, she was completely nude otherwise.

# DESTROYER OF WORLDS

ROYSTON SURVEYED the walls of the massive bunker where his experimental equipment had been installed. The Sector Marshal had tried to insist that someone else be here conducting it, but Royston had put his foot down rather angrily at that suggestion.

The man had only subsided when Royston pointed out that the only other person qualified to handle the machinery was his daughter. It was a low, cruel blow, forcing the man to confront his own cultural chauvinism, but it was still God's honest truth. And Royston didn't always play nice.

As a consolation, they had lengthened many of the cables. It put Royston two meters away from the machinery, instead of lurking over it, but he couldn't see what difference it might make. The radiation involved was not working on anything like an inverse square model here. He would be just as exposed. Just as at risk.

But anything to assuage the Sector Marshal. Alvin obviously feared that losing Royston to an accident would be a blot on his career that nothing would ever remove.

And while he might be right, the Sector Marshal had nothing he could actually do here except sign off on the final approvals that made it all happen and let him build this little fortress.

So Royston was standing in a secured, insulated bunker located in the middle of the Arizona desert. Inside walls nearly a meter thick and reinforced with armor cladding over that. Air conditioning kept the space cool and moist, as though he was still at a LaGrange Point station in space.

The machinery on the wooden bench had seen better days. Scars from energy, chemistry, and brute force had left their marks on the glossy, black surface. Two power cables thicker than his arm passed through holes in the wall on his right and went off to the massive generators that had been installed nearby outside.

There were no other humans within fifteen miles at this point, so if he did manage to blow himself up, hopefully nobody else would be hurt in the process.

Oppenheimer had grown apocalyptic in his old age, convinced that he had personally opened the way for the destruction of the world and death of all humanity. Royston had his doubts about this particular theory, and the tools to exploit it, but at the same time, there was that element of risk in the back of his mind.

Certainly, this was possibly the greatest step forward for humanity in centuries. Since Einstein, perhaps.

But Royston was here because someone else had shown him it was possible. Had opened the door in his mind, just as they had opened the portal into Gareth's cabin.

*They* wished to remain anonymous. Whoever they were. And Royston was likely to wander up to their front door and knock at some point soon.

Hopefully, they would be charitable hosts, along the old Nordic model, and not cannibals.

No time like the present.

Royston walked once around the apparatus to confirm everything in his mind.

"Activating power," he said aloud, knowing his words were being communicated to the Sector Marshal via several radio microphones. Possibly a few others. Sir West had suggested that Her Majesty might be listening in surreptitiously, as might an American President and a few others.

This was bigger than one country. Bigger than the Sky Patrol. Possibly bigger than all of Earth Force.

A small rocker switch had been installed on the right. He flipped it now, and listened to the machine slowly hum to itself.

"We read power on, Doctor Loughty," a man's voice replied quickly. "Edging towards the high end, but still within the band you set previously."

Royston grinned silently. Those bands had been picked arbitrarily. To use the vulgar vernacular, a SWAG. *Scientific Wild-Ass Guess.*

Half of his theory would need to be revised and refined after this, in light of experimental observations. By him if he survived. By Pippa otherwise. But which half was the question to explore.

Royston moved to study the two big gauges set in the face of the machine. Both read zero right now.

He stepped close and turned a dial slowly, watching the needles begin to move, ever so slightly. Again, *SWAG*. Not that he could ever tell anyone that. Except perhaps Sir West. That man understood the nature of pushing the edges of an envelope.

The air took on a golden hue around him as the machine's quiet hum built up to a low C on a concert grand piano.

"Radiation readings at one point eight, Dr. Loughty," the man said aloud. "Stable. Nothing dangerous detected on other bands."

No, there wouldn't be. Either it would work perfectly, or it would fail. Or he would somehow open a portal large enough to annihilate the Earth, and do it so quickly that nobody was likely to notice.

There was that.

He adjusted the knob one last time, getting right to two point zero and letting it hum to itself for several seconds before it decided it was happy.

So far, so good.

Royston moved around to the long end of the bench and studied the Rube Goldberg contraption that his young engineers had made for him. A simple, elevated track starting at shoulder height and running straight and true for about four feet, to a spot eleven inches above the table top itself, where a final curve would bounce the marble coming off the tracks onto the work top.

That much was Newtonian. Almost Galliliean. Simple and safe.

At the far end of the bench, a bowl had been placed. White porcelain with a blue flower pattern around the rim. Six inches deep and a twelve across.

Someone's wife or mother might miss it, come fall when it was time to make casseroles again.

Royston addressed himself to the set of switches installed here. These were larger. They reminded him of mad science in ancient horror movies from the early cinema era. The kind you grabbed with your whole hand and slammed shut like a gunshot.

Hopefully, they had just run out of rocker switches in the construction, and it wasn't the case that someone was making a socio-political statement on Royston's work.

Not that he would blame them, for this truly was mad science.

And yet…

With his left hand, Royston reached into the pocket of his tweed jacket and pulled out a simple marble. A catseye he had owned for fifty-some years. Just the right thing for this.

It grounded him.

"Activating primary power," he said to history.

With his right, Royston took hold of the first switch's handle and closed it.

Somewhere nearby, the generators would come to a higher level of activity, preparing to feed their enormous river of power into the ravenous beast before him.

The lights flickered ominously, but Royston was prepared for that. At least in his mind. If he lost all lights, he had a pocket flash he could pull out. And the doors were locked from the inside with simple mechanical devices, rather than electronics.

The golden hue in the air was brighter now. The air had a smell of ozone and something else he couldn't place. Almost sweet, but that made no sense at all, except as a detail to be noted for later.

"Initiating portals," Royston announced grimly.

It was hard keeping a note of triumphalism out of his voice. Especially since Sir West was standing in the other bunker with Pippa and the Sector Marshal. Doubting, as the man would.

Still, this would be like being whacked upside the head with a four-days-rotting sand shark, if it worked. Even Sir West would be forced to come around.

Royston closed the second big switch and quickly moved to the last one. The guillotine. He was poised to kill the machine at the instant there was a problem. Probably a flaw in his math in that case, as the mechanical construction had been relatively straight forward and the men he hired to perform it worked frequently in movies, constructing amazingly detailed models and mockups as sets. Their skill and professionalism was not to be doubted.

A glowing, golden dinner plate opened beneath the ramp in front of him. Four inches above the surface of the workbench. Possibly eight inches across, and barely one deep, except that Royston suspected he would see infinity if he looked down. Like lining two mirrors up and watching reflections of reflections.

If he dared.

Across the way, a matching golden glow as a reciprocal plate opened.

He hoped.

"Releasing the payload," Royston said as he placed his catseye on the track and let go.

It rolled happily down the middle of the metal

tubes, slowly accelerating, until it hit the curve and plummeted six inches into eternity.

A heartbeat passed. Rapid, yes, but measurable, still.

A tinkling thump as a catseye marble emerged at the far end of the workbench and bounced once, before rattling loosely around the bottom to bleed off inertia.

Royston had been holding his breath. He released it now and watched the future explode out of his mind to reshape humanity.

It was a heady load, but he had done it. This was not the conquest of the entire galaxy, but he could see it from here.

Like Jim Ryan breaking the four minute mile centuries ago, this was as much a psychological hurdle as a scientific one. Others would suddenly have their blinders removed and would no doubt expand and improve on his theory.

But he had just teleported a marble across the length of a workbench, without it seeming to cross the space in between. Technically, he had connected the two points via a fifth-dimensional structure that acted like the inside of a half-torus, in layman's terms. Dig a tunnel underground from A to B and emerge over there.

"Dr. Loughty, is everything all right?" the technician at the other end grew concerned. "Respond, please."

"I'm here," he finally managed to say. "The experiment was a success."

He cut the power feeds and powered the device back down without lobotomizing it in the process, and the walked over to retrieve that marble.

It was a lucky one. That was why he had traded two silverfish and a bloodstone to Tommy Wilson for it, when they were both six and those sorts of things were important.

He would need that luck.

In the back of his mind, Royston expected that he had just grasped the lamp and had summoned forth a djinn.

# IMPOSTER

TO BE SAFEST, at least in his mind, Gareth had insisted on a semi-public dinner, rather than having Diệu Ahn get room service delivered to one of their suites. Where she could have him privately.

She had indeed been sunbathing nude, but had transformed herself into an ingénue when she saw the effect her nudity had on Gareth. Which had somehow made it worse, as she pulled a beach towel into place, mostly, when standing.

Gareth had found himself staring rudely, hoping to catch glimpses of the things he had forbidden himself, like a teenage boy again.

It hadn't helped that she was Borren. Eight feet tall to his seven. Skinny, like a praying mantis. Perhaps a giraffe was more appropriate, when he considered the elaborate pattern of freckles that covered her *entire* body, most of which he had now seen.

She had a tiny jaw and a beautiful smile. Small nostrils emerged at the bottom of a flat, plate nose that extended up to smoothly integrate with her forehead. Hers irises were a green/gray color he found fascinating, especially with black eyeballs. And her eyes were set at angles, low at the inner bottom of an invisible box, and high at the outer corner. Twin ridges of bone and skin served the save purpose as eyebrows, he presumed.

Diệu Ahn, like all Borren, had fine hairs on her skin, like a human woman, but no other hair on her body. Just the various freckles like a giraffe's camouflage.

And a pretty smile.

She wore red tonight. A long tunic dress, almost a sundress, except it was too tight and she wore nothing under it, as far as he could tell. And as Borren were mammalian, at least her small breasts weren't outlined against the thin fabric of the dress.

For a headpiece, she had gone simple, with a structure that rested on her ears and skull and presented almost as a pillbox hat, done in red and black, with a small fascinator attached that reminded Gareth of an Aztec temple.

Gareth had stayed in his almost-cowboy outfit. He also had a black tie tuxedo and could go white-tie if the situation demanded it, but this one didn't. Or he could find several layers of formality in between with a few hours and the right haberdashery computer system.

The maître-d had seated them on a small, circular platform in the middle of the vast dining room. Where it felt like they were on display. Zoo animals, if you wanted to be rude.

Diệu Ahn ate it up like candy, while Gareth tried to maintain his equilibrium. There was undercover, and there was making such a splashy entrance that everyone might forget why you were here, except to be seen.

And here he was.

"So tell me about her," Diệu Ahn began, as they got seated and the first glass of wine served.

The only glass of wine, as far as Gareth was concerned. He could handle his alcohol, but didn't want to make a mess of himself if he had too much.

"Her?" Gareth answered blankly.

"You're wearing a ring, Gareth," Diệu Ahn smiled warmly at him and pointed with a long finger. "Hopefully that means you've found the woman for you, and it isn't just a cheap trick to keep me from sneaking into your bedroom at night and cuddling up against your back."

Gareth blushed. He didn't think she was joking. And wasn't wanting to find out, either way.

"Philippa Loughty," Gareth said. "Pippa."

"Is she the one?" Diệu Ahn's voice got serious.

"I hope so," Gareth replied. "My job takes me away for very long stretches of time, so I don't get to see her. At times, I hope she'll wait for me. But there are other times I wonder if she'd be better off finding someone else and settling down without me."

"Settle down, perhaps," Diệu Ahn said knowingly. "She wouldn't be better off."

More blush as the implications of her words struck home.

"So what brings you to *Morthri*?" Diệu Ahn picked up the conversation rather than letting them dwell in bad places.

Gareth brightened up immediately.

"Partly, my boss sent me on something of a

vacation," he said. It was even more or less true. "Partly, she was intrigued that I might be able to contact you and finagle my way into your world for a time, where I could then be able to write some interesting pieces about the lives of the decadently wealthy. Her readers like that element of living vicariously."

"I see," Diệu Ahn pouted slightly. "So you didn't just come to see me?"

"Not just," Gareth let his tone grow soft. "You are still only the third woman I've ever kissed."

"Really?" that brought her back out of her shell quickly. "Such a disgrace. A handsome Vanir like you should have had his pick of the litter. All the litters."

Gareth shrugged. Part of his cover was to leave out pieces of his own backstory, but let the rest stand on its own. That way, you didn't have to keep track of the lies you had told later.

"When I was younger, I wanted to be a cop," Gareth said. "Worked my ass off for it. Even succeeded for a time, but then everything went wrong. Now, I'm just trying to get my life back on track, and find a way to make a difference in other ways."

"Unknown writer and occasional secret agent?" she asked, taking him back to his excuse for abandoning her on *Orgoth Vortai*.

"Something like that," he acknowledge glumly. That part wasn't even forced.

"Pity you wouldn't be happy as a kept man, Gareth," Diệu Ahn smiled at him, licking her lips carefully. "And hopefully, Pippa will wait. But in the meantime, I think we can have some fun. When was the last time you had a true vacation from work?"

Gareth picked up his wine glass and took a sip as he did math in his head.

"Eleven years," he answered honestly. "Just before I went off to school, I had an entire summer to myself."

"And what did you do?" she was intrigued.

"Built a cabin in the woods, on some land my family owns," he replied, letting his mind drift back. "Split the logs and fit them into the frame. Roofed it and then finished the interior from the shell inwards. Planted a garden for my mother. Swam in the lake when the day got too hot. Hiked when I didn't want to work."

"And that's your idea of a vacation, Gareth?" she was somewhere between amused and appalled, depending on how close the actual work part got to her.

"No, that's what I do when left to my own devices," he corrected her with a grin. "I have no idea how to actually vacation."

"Well, then," she raised her own glass in a toast that Gareth matched. "We'll just have to see what we can do to broaden your horizons."

They drank and smiled at each other as the waitress approached.

It would get him connected to a whole new stratum and element of society. The richest ones.

Grodray had insisted that most were good little *Accord* citizens, and that many of the so-called crimes he might encounter around them were barely worth noting in passing. But at the same time, the money to fund the criminal underworld in the galaxy had to come from somewhere.

Gareth was a bloodhound now, seeking a scent.

GENERAL

MARC and his inner crew had returned to the planet *Kani*. It made a helpful place to hide. Like when he was here six months ago, they had managed to rent an entire vacation resort area as a place to rest and work. That one had been in the midst of a major forested area.

Now, they were in their own desert, it felt like. In the cool and rainy season, this place was wall-to-wall with tourists and campers hiking hither and yon. But this was the high summer on *Kani* at this latitude, and it didn't get below thirty degrees Celsius at night, running up above forty routinely during the day.

That was okay. His Vanir body could tolerate that level of heat far better than his human one had. And the Warreth as a rule didn't start to lose mental efficiency until things got above forty-five degrees.

Only the Nari really complained. Well, the younger ones. Zorge commented that he was always cold as an old man, so the extra heat made him comfortable. The kids needed toughening, anyway.

So Marc had brought everyone to a resort for a month. Toughen them up, like Zorge said, by making them hike and exercise in heat. Put them through something like he had done in basic training, when he joined Sky Patrol. Make soldiers out of them, instead of just hired thugs. Washing out here meant demotion, since Marc was going to form his elite out of the survivors.

That meant everyone worked that much harder.

Today, Marc was on a mesa with Zorge, Maiair, and Yooyar, plus a few of the more science-minded of his crew: a couple of Nari and three Warreth troopers.

Mishalska, one of the Nari, had gone so far in this heat as to clip most of his tan fur extremely short, and then buzz strange patterns into the remainder, like tribal markings. The young man was standing close by, acting as a bodyguard today with a beam rifle held point down and eyes constantly in motion.

In the distance, a flying truck was approaching, beginning to circle prior to touching down.

"Is it safe?" Maiair asked quietly from close by.

"There are risks," Marc answered. "But we need to take them at this point."

She withdrew a few steps and drew her own pistol from the holster on her thigh, looking now like a copy of her younger sister, with both of them armed and alert. Both wore heavy cotton pants in taupe, with black hiking boots, and bikini tops in red that matched their feathers.

The Warreth had originally been uplifted by the Chaa from a creature similar to an emu, back on

*Earth.* The Gods had transformed them into bipedal mammals that gave birth to live young, rather than egg-layers, when they patterned them similar to the Vanir, but they still had feathers covering their skin and providing communicative head feathers and short beaks instead of lips.

And they were both killers. That was all Marc really cared about.

The truck dropped down finally and landed with a small whirlwind of dust kicked up as it settled.

A man stepped out of the passenger side with a smile.

"Maximus, it is good to see you," he said.

Gonquah was Th'Tarni. On most worlds where they lived, the species formed something of a culturally- and socially-oppressed minority. Marc could understand why.

The man was short. Just over five feet tall, so short even for them. He had dark skin that was rough, almost like tree bark, and covered on his neck and the sides of his face with freckles that glowed with their own internal light, as did the eyes that had no iris or pupil, just a baby blue ball of fire staring out. His hair, like others, was black, pulled back and kept long, coming down to tips that looked more like leaves than anything, flat like blades with internal structures. And glowing with the same blue at the tips, edges, and roots.

Gonquah's kind were unsettling to look at, but Marc had seen worse in his time.

He stepped up to Gonquah and shook the tiny man's hand carefully.

"Do you have a prize for me, Gonquah?" Marc asked.

"Indeed, Maximus," he beamed. "Come and see."

The man led Marc and many of the others around to the back of the truck, a tarp-covered flatbed filled with several boxes the size and shape of coffins. Two more Th'Tarni waited back here, dressed in what looked like paramilitary uniforms to Marc's experienced eye.

"Open one up," Gonquah commanded.

One of the troopers unlatched a lid and flipped it open, reaching in and doing something.

The being inside sat up. Machine.

It was Marc's android, as he had designed it, except the face was alien. Two eyes, wideset to give it hunter's vision. A mouth from which words could emerge. Ears on both sides human enough. A steel helmet of a skull perhaps, on a steel skeleton designed to elicit panic among humans with superstitions. And most of the rest of the *Accord*, from what Marc had studied.

"Arise," Gonquah ordered the machine.

The android stood and stepped out of the box on careful feet.

"Come," the Th'Tarni continued.

The machine man leapt gracefully to the ground, but still made a racket when he landed. All steel and power systems.

Gonquah pointed at Marc with one hand.

"Maximus is your owner," Gonquah said. "Acknowledge."

The machine turned to Marc and studied him briefly.

"Maximus," it said in a dry, metallic voice and a quick bow of the head. "Acknowledged."

"What is your task, creature?" Marc asked loud enough that everyone could hear.

"To guard you, master," the robot said. "To follow your orders."

Marc reached down to the holster on his thigh and drew the beam pistol. It was just a stun model, but could have easily been something lethal. He handed it to the robot, watched the machine man take it in one hand comfortably, turning the weapon sideways briefly to check the safety and power level.

"Shoot those three," Maximum commanded, pointing at two Warreth males and a Nari.

The machine immediately snapped off three shot as fast as the pistol would cycle.

Amazingly, Mishalska managed to dodge to his right, nearly getting his rifle up to shoot back before the machine caught him with a fourth bolt that dropped him.

"Any others, master?" the android asked politely.

"No." Marc laughed, watching the utter shock play out on the other faces around him.

Most of the other faces. Zorge had only been a little surprised. Maiair and Yooyar were grinning. Gonquah's smile could have lit up the night.

"I take it this meets with your approval, Maximus?" the arms merchant asked with a feral smile. "I'm rather looking forward to making more for you. Perhaps a small army, once you have a chance to test these four out and refine anything that needs adjusting."

"And why is that. Gonquah?" Marc asked.

He knew the truth. Had done extensive research on the topic and the man before selecting the young industrialist personally for the manufacturing task.

Gonquah was a dedicated revolutionary. An angry young man willing to use the wealth he had inherited to build an arms manufacturing capability disguised as a white good factory. Killer robots instead of refrigerators, as it were.

"Because the Vanir have ruled us long enough, Maximus," the little man said. "Barring yourself, they need to be cast down from their privileged heights to live as my kind have been forced to for fifty thousand years."

Yes. Angry. A welcome fellow-traveler. A man who would help him break the Constabulary and the *Accord* itself.

Too bad he wouldn't live to enjoy the fruits of his labor, but Marc was thinking in centuries now.

"So, my friend," Marc said. "I will need a month or three to put these machines through their paces. And then we will have a nice, private dinner somewhere and discus the future."

"Indeed, my troublesome ally," Gonquah clapped him on the arm and returned to the truck. "I look forward to it."

The men unloaded the other three coffins and four robots took up their places in a line.

Marc had left his stunner on the lowest setting, so the three targets of his demonstration were stirring as the truck flew away.

Marc walked over to Mishalska and helped the man to his feet with a big paw.

"Impressive, Mishalska," Marc said with a friendly smile. "You shouldn't have been able to even react, let alone move. What other things can you do to astound me?"

"Just you wait, sir," the young man said, a little groggily.

Marc nodded. A month of hard training would make these men and women almost as dangerous as his killer robots.

And then, my friends, let us see how the *Accord* survives.

## FIRST INSPECTOR

"YOU'RE SURE?" the Vanir woman asked, turning to look at the little communications handset on her desk. "We have independent confirmation on this?"

"We do," a male voice came over the intercom line. "They were broadcasting a radio communications signal at the same time, so we were able to synchronize with our scanners picking up the signal."

"And nothing at all was done at the time?" she confirmed, brushing a stray black hair out of her eyes as she concentrated.

"That's correct, First Inspector," the man replied. "Per your orders."

"Very well."

She cut the line and leaned back in her chair to think. Her office suddenly felt claustrophobic, in spite of being large enough to hold fifteen friendly Vanir for a meeting. Or thirty Grace.

Anen Wardson rose from behind her desk and began to pace, glancing occasionally at the early evening sky displayed out the window. From here, the horizon of *Almar* looked almost endless, as fit a world frequently referred to as the Axle of Time.

The capital of the *Accord of Souls*. The platform from which the Chaa themselves had leapt outward, leaving the Vanir behind to try to hold this new galactic civilization together.

Anen was First Inspector. The Commander in Chief of the Constabulary. Not all of them had been Vanir, like her, but many had. The species held a special love for the *Accord*.

A place now threatened by the worst possible thing she could imagine.

On a warm, blue planet, clear out to the edge of the galaxy, a species that hadn't even been above the Stone Age when the Chaa left, had just opened their first wormhole. And done it more than a thousand years before the most ambitiously-paranoid speculation had suggested it was even possible.

It was a threat to the entire galaxy. Xenocidal maniacs let loose from their galactic prison to run roughshod over a place where violence was barely allowed, and war completely unknown.

Xenocide. To wipe out an entire species. Nearly impossible with star-faring technology, but that wouldn't prevent the humans from trying. They took any excuse to kill one another, frequently using skin tone as a distinction.

What would they do when they encountered the Grace? Or the Nari? Or the Borren? To say nothing of the more exotic species that probably factored into Human nightmares such as the Ramasayia or the Arawath.

Still, it was her job to know these things, as well

as to deal with them. First Inspector was the principal law-enforcement agent in a galaxy that hadn't had words for war, until the humans had become a potential threat.

Anen returned to her desk and placed a call.

"Commissioner Diazal's office," a bright, cheerful voice came on immediately. "How may I assist you, First Inspector?"

"I would like you to find me a half hour in the Commissioner's schedule, as soon as possible," Anen replied politely, letting the content of her words convey the immediacy that she dared not spell out, even on an internal line, within the *Accord's* Hall of Government. "Preferably today."

There was a pause she put down to someone clicking hold. It stretched. Probably bouncing this up to the Commissioner's Chief of Staff, if that woman was still in the office.

It was late in the day. Possibly, most of the Commissioner's staff had gone home.

Anen was seventy-one. Her grandchildren would be starting families soon enough, and her current wife, Elloayn, understood the needs of the service, having retired herself five years ago.

A new voice came on the line.

"Hello, Anen," Commissioner Diazal replied in a warm, easy tone.

The Commissioner was known as much for his intellect as his charisma. She needed the former right now. Obviously, he had done the math in his head, when the Prime Investigator of the Constabulary called and requested a meeting.

"Hello, Petim," she replied. "When can we have a chat?"

There. Leave it at that.

Pause. Weighing the things she would not say.

"I was about to head out for some dinner," he offered carefully. "Would you care to join me?"

"Would it be possible to get something delivered, instead?" Anen countered.

She heard the faint catch in the Commissioner's breath.

"Certainly," he decided after a moment. "You order something and get enough for two. Or order me some fish, if you would?"

"That will be lovely, Petim," Anen decided. "I'll be up in a few minutes."

"Yes," his voice fell just a trace. "I was afraid you would say that."

Fortunately, she worked late frequently. There were several places that she could call on, already cleared to deliver food to his floor. A quick message home to Elloayn that she would be much later than expected tonight, and Anen Wardson headed to the lift tube.

The Commissioner's office, when she got up there, was largely dark. One young Borren woman in front, more or less guarding the door. She gestured Anen right through to the back.

Petim's office was lit. It was large enough for meetings, although not as big as hers.

Anen entered with a smile and closed to door.

"That bad?" he asked, rising from behind his desk to greet her.

Petim Diazal was one of the Arawath. Many people had remarked over the centuries that they seemed to be smaller cousins of the Vanir. Tall, slender bipeds with hair on their heads and skin elsewhere. Slightly smaller than Grace overall, or even humans, if you wanted to make that comparison.

Blue skin marked the significant difference, as they were a fully aquatic species that could walk on dry land, as long as they were able to immerse themselves frequently and let clean water run over the gills on either side of the necks.

Today, he wore a muted, russet suit in a herringbone pattern. Expensive and well cut to make him even more impressive.

Petim was short and slender, even for his species. But he had worked hard on his physical presence, and in turn had been elected to the *Accord* Commission at a very young age. A well-deserved accolade, though.

He was not the Proctor of the Commission, but many expected that to happen when the current worthy retired in another few years.

"Sit, please," he said, directing her to a sofa and two chair off to one side.

She chose the closer chair and watched Petim recline on the couch.

"How bad?" he asked after a moment. "What do I need to plan for?"

"Possibly a worst-case scenario, Commissioner," she replied, letting him know that it wasn't just a personal thing, but a business issue.

She watched the man steel himself and swallow once.

"Tell me," he directed her.

"Within the last few days, we have detected, observed, and confirmed the human scientist, Royston Loughty, successfully demonstrating a very primitive, short-range wormhole generator," Anen said. "The humans are possibly within a few generations of breaking out of their home system and threatening the *Accord*."

Even a man with blue skin can pale appreciably, if all the blood drains out of his face. And his diving membranes flickered down over his black eyes once in shock before they withdrew.

"Who knows?" he asked, assuming the report and moving on to the implications.

"Nobody outside of my organization, as yet," Anen replied. "I got off the phone and called you immediately. This will need to be handled with the utmost care and diligence, but at the same time, speed is off the essence."

"Why is that?" Petim asked, suddenly leaning forward and dropping his hands onto his knees.

"Loughty is an unknown quantity," Anen said. "Our wildest fears would be that it would take them only another thousand years to reach a technological sophistication sufficient to even understand wormhole physics," Anen also leaned forward, placing them close enough to almost whisper now. "We're not sure how to stop him, short of considering the ultimate sanction."

Petim recoiled. Assassination was always possible. At one point, the Commission had even explored the necessity of eliminating the humans entirely, using biological warfare to destroy the species while not wiping out all the other life forms.

"Genius?" Petim asked. "Loughty?"

"At least," she said. "And I fear we are partly responsible for the entire thing. I am, personally."

"How?"

"Gareth Dankworth," she reminded him. "His kidnapping by the criminal Maximus seems to have set in motion the chain of events that drove Loughty to consider the higher physics. And then to successfully unravel them well enough to become a threat. I made the decision not to have Gareth transformed back into a human, killed, and returned to Earth, which might have deflected Loughty from this path. In light of events, that might have been a mistake."

Petim blinked again. The Commission generally had clean hands, but only because many decisions had to be made at much lower levels. He was seeing the sausage-making now, probably in ways that had not been quite so clear before.

"Do we destroy the humans?" he asked. Again, the leap of logic, without having to slowly work his way through all the possible dead ends. His snap caused her to flinch. "Just like that? Or somehow stop Loughty?"

"I do not think we can stop Loughty at this point," she replied. "And the technology has been proven successful, so it will metastasize over time. The humans are like that. But this is not my decision to make."

"Indeed, First Inspector," Petim nodded. "Something like this must come from the very top. You will provide the Commission your report how soon?"

"Tomorrow," she said. "If you believe they will be ready to calmly and rationally consider it. Xenocide is a powerful action that cannot be undone later. Nor can assassination."

"No, it cannot, Anen," Petim agreed. "But I have a much greater fear to address."

"What's that?" she asked, wondering what could possibly top something so drastic.

"What happens if the Chaa take exception to the situation and decide to do something about it?"

# VACATION

PERHAPS THERE WAS something to this concept of relaxation.

Gareth stood on the top-most deck, slightly sheltered from the wind as the yacht cut a white swath through the outer harbor. Below, there were at least five different species lounging somewhere on the rear deck in the late morning sun. Male and female. Diệu Ahn was among them, in a red string bikini he wasn't sure had enough material to make him a handkerchief.

The others wore less. Sometimes nothing, in the case of one Nari woman with fur just on the verge of faded mustard. Gareth tried not to stare, but the xenobiologist in him was fascinated by the wide range of humanity below him. And the likenesses.

Except he shouldn't call it humanity. None of them were humans, not even him. Vanir, Borren, Nari, Grace, Ramasaya, even a Moisa which reminded him of an uplifted praying mantis that had four arms hanging from her torso and six legs off of a small abdomen. Like a compact centaur, maybe.

Possibly the weirdest species, to hear the others talk, the Moisa had huge, compound eyes on either sides of her skull, nostril slits inside that, and a tiny mouth. The species were generally herbivores that went heavy on pollen and plant life.

They were the builders. The architects who designed the fantastic hexagonal buildings so common throughout the *Accord*. Gareth had grown up with square buildings and the occasional round tower, but the hexagon was so much prettier, especially when the Moisa went to such effort to make them blend in, like a forest of giant trees masquerading as a city.

As Gareth listened to the quiet churn of the big twin propellers driving the massive yacht forward, he wondered about the Chaa. They had uplifted sixteen other species at the same time they downgraded the Vanir, setting everyone on a rough parity that had lasted for at least fifty thousand years before he and Maximus came along.

No war. Very little disease. No hunger.

Poverty, if it existed, was contained as well.

He had seen representations of the Elders. Usually Grace interpretations, so done with some level of artistic license or bombast.

Erect biped with bilateral symmetry, assuming the Vanir had looked the most like them before. Human-like, to most degrees of classification, with only the pointed ears and greater scale truly marking the species different, at least externally.

If one thing stood out, it was that the Vanir were

always so much bigger than everyone else. Borren might be taller, but they were spindly enough that he was always afraid he would hurt Diệu Ahn while dancing. The other species were all done to human scale, more or less. A few were half that size.

If a Grace covered their hair, he was pretty sure one could walk the streets of New Metropolis, or maybe Shangdu and nobody would notice.

He wondered if one ever had.

"Enjoying the day?" a voice intruded on Gareth as he day-dreamed.

Gareth turned to see a much smaller man standing next to him. Gonquah was Th'Tarni, a species he couldn't help but think of as wood elves. The dangerous pixies of European legend, living in the forest and playing tricks on humans. Five and half feet tall with black hair that had glowing blue at the ends and roots, and matching eyes and freckles.

"Absolutely," Gareth smiled and shook the proffered hand. "I can't remember the last time I was actually on vacation. Normally, I'm on assignment here or there, and too busy paying attention to my surroundings to actually enjoy them."

"I understand," the man laughed and turned to watch the bevy of beauties on his boat's fantail. "Diệu Ahn tells me you are a reporter?"

The voice sounded just a little off. Like maybe he thought Gareth was a muckraker gone undercover to expose crime and corruption to sell papers? Which was kinda the truth, at the end of the day. Maybe.

"Fashion and art," Gareth stuck with his cover story. "High end magazines with limited subscription bases, rather than the red tops. The glossies that let wealthy people show off and make other wealthy people jealous. Or let the average Jane dream about marrying a prince."

"Oh," he suddenly turned much brighter and chuckled. "Then remind me to take you on a full tour of my little boat, so you can make all the others unhappy. Got dinner plans later when we get back to dock?"

Gareth shrugged.

"I'm here as Diệu Ahn's Plus One," he nodded. "At some point next week, my editor expects me to check in, but I don't have to be on my next mission for at least another week after that."

"Good, Gareth," Gonquah decided, snapping his fingers. "You two will dine with me tonight and we can talk politics."

"Oh, I never talk politics," Gareth warned.

"All art is politics," Gonquah grinned up at him.

"And those conversations are even worse," Gareth allowed a small chuckle. "The statue at the top of the *Accord* Hall of Arts entryway sums it up greater than anything else I've ever seen."

"*The Art Critic*, yes," Gonquah agreed. "But I'm sure you have a much different outlook on those sorts of things than most of the people I encounter regularly. Either they are businesspeople whose only art is the hustle, or people like Diệu Ahn, who never bother with the business end and just let their portfolio managers handle everything. I would be interested in an outsider's take."

"I can try," Gareth offered. "So what do you do for money, Gonquah? You seem to fall somewhere in between those two groups."

"My father was much older than normal when I was born," the man's glowing blue eyes shifted to focus on the blue horizon. "I inherited his vast business empire just out of school, and have spent the last decade adjusting its focus. He was content to just serve the frivolous desires of the common people."

"And you?" Gareth asked.

"I want to change the *Accord*, Gareth," the Th'Tarni man turned a serious face back this direction. "It has grown stale and predictable. All the old lines have calcified. It's time to shake things up."

Gareth grunted and nodded, but remained silent. After a moment, Gonquah smiled and headed forward again, down the steps to the main cabin and bidding him adieu until later.

Something about his tones had Gareth's back up. This didn't sound like a simple suggestion of a new fashion trend. No, it had felt like a call to arms. He made a note to ask Diệu Ahn a few misleading questions to see if she had any background on the man. Most of the people he had met in the last few days were like Gonquah had said. Either hustlers chasing after business or *bon vivants* with so much money that eventually it turned into oxygen, something you only noticed by its absence.

Gonquah might be something else.

<hr>

SUNSET FOUND them atop the tallest tower in Narvanie, the capital city of the world. Gonquah's penthouse spanned an entire city block, because the

Moisa who had designed this building had narrowed it at the waist, like a tree, before swelling it back out at the canopy.

Gareth had been able to look straight down from slanted windows at the world below, so far away that even the auto-taxis looked like ants.

It was not an impromptu dinner party, as several other couples had joined, some from the boat and some just meandering in. If pressed, Gareth would have called it an open, rolling party, running all day, and centered on Gonquah's presence. The man felt like that. The situation felt like that.

The mob were all scattered around the suite now, having consumed a wide buffet meal, rather than sitting in formal elegance with salad forks. But Gareth and Diệu Ahn had ended up in a smaller, homier salon with the tannish Nari woman from the boat and a Ramasayia male whose name Gareth had missed, then been too embarrassed to ask later.

The Ramasayia reminded him of nothing so much as an Australian wombat, with a fine gray-brown fur covering their body and expressive eyes, plus a nose that never seemed to stop twitching, as if it was tasting the room more than watching it. And he had a pouch, where Gareth watched him pull out a pocket comm, type something, and then stuff it back in. In spite of the pockets on his loose pants and vest.

Gareth thought jealously about all the times he could have used a stomach pouch.

"So Gareth," Gonquah's voice pulled him back to the present. "Where is art going to be in say, five years' time?"

The man's eyes had an odd gleam to them as

Gareth swished the glass of something he had been nursing for the last hour. He looked at the far wall and let his eyes wander, taking in the expensive silk paintings, the rich ornamentation on flat surfaces, and the books all leather-bound on a case nearby.

This wasn't just a general question. No, it was a test. A chance to out him as a fraud, perhaps, when what it might really do it suggest he was a cop, if he answered it wrong. That was the tone of voice Gareth had picked up. And Diệu Ahn, as well, as she leaned close and put her weight on his arm, seeming to distract him as he looked up and smiled at her.

"I'll go out on a limb and suggest that the Alternative Realism School work will begin to be considered too pedestrian in another year," Gareth said, zeroing in the on the man. "Everyone will have a collection of some flavor, and it will lose that element of exclusivity and cache that it has now. You'll see cheap knockoffs starting to show up in middle class catalogs by then."

"And what replaces it?" the Th'Tarni pressed. "What can I buy now that sets a trend everyone else will have to pay extra to emulate when they arrive too late?"

Gareth smiled. There was always that. The man wanted to show everyone else up by beating them to the punch. But why ask a stranger? Unless you suspected him of being deeper than just an interested observer.

Sure. Let's play.

"I know an artist working on *Yuudix*," Gareth said evenly, somehow sensing everyone as they leaned forward to catch his words, afraid that they might miss out. "A Moisa woman whose name eludes me now but I could look her up in my contacts list later. She's doing ultra-miniature cities, one building at a time, each custom designed for an overall aesthetic to fit the space into which it will be viewed."

"How miniature?" Gonquah asked, dollar signs suddenly appearing, however metaphorically in his eyes.

Gareth held up his right hand and measured four centimeters between his thumb and forefinger.

"This tower," Gareth said, "Maybe a little bigger. I only got to hear about her from someone else, and see some two-D pictures and one blurry hologram she had produced as a simple advertisement. She forbids most photography, but these had been captured in the background while snapping stills of her in her studio. They were blown up and indistinct, but took my breath away, even then."

Gareth felt a spike of conscience run through him like a frozen knife. But her work had been amazing, and she was working on the very fringes of art on *Yuudix*, a world more focused on science than the pleasurable pursuits. It had been a background interview someone in the Constabulary had done, and she had mentioned scraping by on a regular basis, subsisting on the Universal Basic Income and living cheap, so as to have time for her dreams.

From the hungry look in Gonquah's eyes, she would be getting a call soon, and probably an offer no sane artist would turn down. Hopefully, success wouldn't completely ruin her life. But at least she would have that choice. And a lot of people attached to this party, or even in this room, making inquiries about prior pieces and available prices.

Art made no sense, except that it made the artist happy to create, and the buyer happy to own. And Gareth was tired of bombastic bronzes of super-life-sized godlings.

It reminded him of the stranger he saw in the mirror in the morning.

"Is it truly that impressive?" Gonquah breathed in apparently disbelief. "Her cityscapes?"

Gareth shrugged eloquently. She had been ignored by the major schools of art as being too far out there, but there was so much money sloshing around, just in this room, that she could live comfortably on a few commissions and survive when the wheels of interest turned to something even more bizarre, five years after that.

He hoped she would eventually forgive him. The people around him looked like they wanted to bolt the room so they could make private inquiries one step ahead of everyone else.

He suspected the party would end up moving to *Yuudix* tomorrow somehow. Possibly the day after. He wondered if Diệu Ahn would accompany it, trying to slice off a piece for herself a rock-bottom prices today.

Gonquah pulled a device from the inside pocket of his dinner jacket and pressed a button.

"This calls for a toast," he said into the thing, apparently. "Five glasses of champagne delivered."

"Arriving shortly," a female voice replied. Except it sounded mechanical rather than organic.

Gonquah slid the device back into his pocket and smiled at everyone.

"I have a surprise for everyone tonight," he announced in a broad, conspiratorial voice.

"Something completely new that I'll be offering shortly from one of my factories."

Everyone waited on pins and needles.

A mechanical man entered the room, carrying five flutes on a tray. The people around Gareth all cooed and squawked with surprise.

It was about six feet tall. Looked like a robot from a bad scifi vid to Gareth, with thin arms and legs, and big joints. The surface reminded him of nickel steel with a satin finish. The face was human-enough, as well, with eyes, nose, and mouth, plus ears, but they looked like something you drew with simple geometric shapes rather than having a Grace or Moisa artist do the work.

It paused in front of Gonquah and bowed, lowering the tray until everyone took a glass.

"What in the name of Zaffan is that?" Diệu Ahn asked. "Some kind of mechanical being?"

"I was commissioned to begin production of them by a Vanir designer," Gonquah said. "It is indeed a mechanical servant. He called it an *Android*."

Gareth hoped he kept his flinch deep inside, where nobody else would detect it. Even Diệu Ahn seemed focused on the new arrival, so he prayed she was too distracted.

*Android* was a human word. And Gareth could only think of one Vanir that would use it.

It frightened him to consider what an android might do here, where they could be programmed to do anything the owner desired. Anything. Just like back home.

That included turning into an army of killer robots.

Because Marc Sarzynski was the only other person Gareth could think of who would know that word. And he was a Vanir.

How much worse would that man be next time?

# VINDICATED

ROYSTON HAD NEVER BEEN INVITED to the palace as an individual. He had certainly attended significant events here, but only as part of a larger group.

Not one where he was the guest of honor. Worse, he was being escorted today by an extremely mature, fourteen-year-old Crown Prince Henry, as they traversed these ancient hallways, teeming with history and culture dating back more than a millennia in many places.

Henry was a ninety-percent-sized copy of his father, the Prince Consort, and would probably grow into his full height in another year. Right now Royston had an inch on the young prince, but that would change. His father was nearly six foot three.

They were both dressed professionally today. This was not a major, public ceremony, to be witnessed by friends and cameras. Instead, a polite Tea was happening. As Henry opened a door and ushered Royston through with a hand.

Inside, Prince Daniel, the Royal Consort, tall and fit. A man who still played polo regularly in season, and showed his service in the Household Guards in his erect carriage. Indeed, young Henry would follow in his footsteps in another few years, unless he chose to do his service in Earth Force Sky Patrol instead, which would be a welcome first for this ancient family.

The other two children, Sarah and Emily, were too young to attend today, Royston presumed, being eleven and nine, but would no doubt grow up just as involved as their older brother.

Sir West was here already, seated to one side in a suit that showed all the hallmarks of having been freshly pressed. Possibly the suit he wore solely to the palace, and no other time, so that it didn't smell of tobacco or have stains from whatever Sir West had eaten most recently.

Her Majesty rose to shake Royston's hand as he was presented. Elizabeth III, Queen of England. She was a tall, willowy blond approaching forty. A long face with a prominent nose could have rendered her homely, but the high cheekbones offset that in such a way to convey a raptor's face instead. Especially when those blue eyes focused on you.

Like now.

The Prince Consort served tea steeped to the perfect thickness, into exquisite porcelain cups. The Queen first. The Crown Prince. Sir West. And then Royston himself. Just a mathematician and physicist, as it were.

At least today.

This meeting might change all that.

The small talk had eventually evaporated, like the

little sandwiches and the first mugs of tea. Now they were into the second round. Where things would get interesting.

Her Majesty had a cold, intellectual gleam in her eyes as she blew on her second cup of tea and studied Royston. He felt like a dormouse awaiting the chef's pleasure. The door to the chamber was closed, and locked.

"Prince Henry has recently begun to study advanced sciences, Mister Loughty," she began in an offhand way, gesturing to the youngest member of the group.

The young man blushed awkwardly, but that was probably the fact that such studies would not doubt include reading one of his books and three to five of Sir West's, depending on the field studied. And the young man was having tea with them today by way of introduction.

Royston nodded politely to both of them. She hadn't asked a question, nor invited a comment.

"He has also recently begun to be more active in the affairs of the Household, so that he can represent Us in public in the future," she continued. "So I thought it appropriate that he join us to discuss your most recent activities."

"Just so, Your Majesty," Royston replied carefully.

She probably knew more about his experiments than even Sir West did, because the security classification around it would be that high. But as supreme executive of one of the founding members of Earth Force, she could pull rank, if someone like Royston had suggested to Sir West that she do just such a thing, as he had. The PM was the only other person who could do that, and that worthy was really a shopkeeper from Scunthorpe at the end of the day. Not a physicist. Nor a Queen.

"I understand you were successful, Mr. Loughty," she dangled the bait in front of him expertly.

"We were, madam," he replied, carefully taking note of his language that it never grew too personal. Sir West could possibly call the woman by her Christian name in private, but he had known her since she was Emily's age, at least. "The theory bears out soundly, but now I must go back and revise the paper, in light of experimental evidence. Some of my assumptions were simply wrong. Others were too cautious. But we can press forward in careful steps."

"How soon do you envision building a larger device, Mr. Loughty?" she asked, eyes boring in on him.

Royston leaned back carefully, paying extra attention to his body language as he did. This was where things would get interesting.

Whoever hosted the first large transporter machine would have a significant political and economic edge over the rest of the planet. And the solar system as well, if goods and personnel could instantly move from London to the Neptunian mining colonies without requiring transit time and delta-v burn calculations. It would open up the entire solar system in ways that not even the jet airliner had done to the surface of the globe, centuries ago.

"That is contingent on two things," Royston replied judiciously. "One, the entire apparatus will need to be dismantled and examined by specialists to make sure there are no issues inside that will cause us problems when we scale things up. And two, budgetary constraints. This task is currently being handled as part of Earth Force Sky Patrol, related to certain internal investigations they are pursuing."

"Yes, the disappearance of Field Agent Gareth St. John Dankworth from his cabin aboard the Arsenal," she acknowledged smartly. "I understand that the Americans are deeply interested in that aspect of your research. And contemplating that he may have been kidnapped by forces currently unknown on *Earth*."

Royston couldn't help but glance at the other three men in the room, counting the young Crown Prince as grown up enough to be involved, if his mother shared that opinion.

Her words suggested that she had followed his original train of thought. That a previously-unknown alien species had kidnapped the man. But why Gareth? And why do it in such a public place? There were many others that could have been taken instead, and done in such a way that perhaps nobody would even have noticed.

"And I have cleared everyone in this room to discuss any sensitive materials related to Dankworth, Mr. Loughty," she continued in a voice forged of steel.

She could do that. As Head of State, it was within her ancient prerogatives to appoint her own advisors, which had long included Sir West on the scientific side. And presumably the Prince Consort so that she had someone outside of the formal government at close call.

"I have a theory, Your Majesty," Royston offered diffidently after a moment to gather this errant thoughts together and lick his lips. "I cannot lend any scientific credence to the claim, but at the same time I also cannot refute any portion of it, using the old standards of Doyle and Holmes."

"Go on," she said in a breathless tongue.

"Gareth was kidnapped by removing him through such a wormhole as I have now proven can be constructed and used," Royston turned deadly serious. "No one else in this solar system was, at the time, capable of replicating the feat, as far as I, and by extension Earth Force, have been able to tell."

"In this solar system?" Prince Consort Daniel spoke up now for the first time, the military officer in him coming to the fore. "Did I understand you correctly?"

"You do, sir," Royston nodded to him. "My pet theory is that he was taken by an unknown alien species from outside our sphere."

"But why?" young Prince Henry spoke up. "Why him? Why then? Why there?"

"It is the *when* that drives my theory, young sir," Royston said. "Sir West and I have spoken in loose terms about it before now, only because he is not a member of any Earth Force Directorate at present, so I could not share certain classified details with him before this moment. But Gareth is, was, one of the top agents in Sky Patrol. A hero, if you will. I have an irrational theory that whoever it was had identified him as the person they needed, perhaps for some heroic task elsewhere. Had you known the man, you would understand. But they needed him at a specific moment in time. That he was alone in his cabin was just luck on their part, as they might have just as easily taken him while he was at dinner, and the event witnessed by dozens, or potentially hundreds of people."

"So you ascribe benevolence to them?" Her Majesty's tone was tart.

"I do not necessary ascribe malice, Your Majesty, which is not the same thing," Royston carefully corrected her assumption. "It all comes down to *why Gareth* and *why then*. Whoever it was could have just as easily taken other men whose disappearance would raise no fuss."

"Have they taken others?" Prince Henry asked suddenly. "Do we have other men missing who might fit the characteristics, the circumstances you have identified? Whom we have not previously associated with the disappearance of this agent?"

Royston remembered to close his mouth before any flies took up residence. The two proud parents beamed. Even Sir West grinned at his shock, having previously remained a touch aloof from the whole event that was Royston's presentation to the Crown.

"It strikes me that if they have the confidence to capture this one man, it might not be their first attempt," the young prince continued carefully. "Who else have they taken?"

"I do not know the answer to that, sir," Royston admitted, shocked almost out of his wits by the penetrating question. "But I intend to task certain people with looking into that exact question when I return to the Arsenal. I may have missed the forest for the trees. Thank you."

He nodded gratefully to the boy, the young man, who was blushing furiously now.

"Well done, Henry," his mother rescued him. "Now, Mr. Loughty, let us return to the other topic. The question of budget, as to where the first large-scale demonstration project of your engine might be constructed."

"Indeed, Your Majesty," he replied,

They began to discuss locations and costs, but Royston's mind kept circling back to that one question that might answer why Gareth had been taken at the time he was.

Who else had gone before?

# SECRET AGENT MAN

THEY HAD RETURNED to the hotel late in the evening. Or early in the morning, depending on how you wanted to look at it.

Gareth figured the sun would rise in about two hours, given the lightening sky in the east, so he should have gone to bed a long time ago. These people liked to follow the darkness, rather than the day.

Diệu Ahn had invited him up to her suite for a nightcap, but it was clear she wasn't using that as a thin veil for a proposed romp. She had gotten a little withdrawn and pensive over the last few hours as he had watched the Borren woman.

They sat on her balcony now and watched the night sky now, across a low table from each other in comfie canvas sling-chairs and covered with light blankets against the chill. Gareth had made himself a simple hot chocolate. Diệu Ahn had originally planned on something stronger, but the smell turned her head, and she had done the same, with a small shot of something like apple schnapps in hers.

He would already sleep well, just from the exhaustion of a twenty-seven hour day. And he was safe here, as he could simply climb over the low rail separating the balconies and get into his suite if he didn't feel like the long stroll inland and back to go something like fifteen feet.

"Is everything okay?" he finally broached the topic as they settled in the dimness and cool breeze off the water.

Nothing more. Leave it at that. He had never learned how human women thought, and Diệu Ahn was both alien and from a radically different socio-economic background from him. They might be talking foreign languages, depending. Plus, he didn't want to pry.

"Is she real?" Diệu Ahn asked.

"Is who real?" Gareth sipped his mug and tried to figure out which conversation they were having. Never an easy chore with some women.

"That artist you mentioned tonight," she said, still pensive. "The one who makes miniature cityscapes."

"Oh, her," Gareth nodded, glad that the woman didn't want to talk about Pippa right now. "Yes, she's real. And hopefully, if she ever finds out about me, and tonight, she'll forgive me for sending people with a lot of money after her."

"Why is that, Gareth?" she probed.

"The woman is an artist," he said. "I read a thing on her and it included her desire for more support, but she was really only looking for a few people willing to buy her work and tell their friends. I've possibly put her on magazine covers as the *Next Big Thing*. It might ruin her life."

"We call that failing upward," she smiled in the shadows, teeth suddenly flashing and disappearing from otherwise darker skin. "I had wondered because…"

She stopped there. Just hung the phrase like she had run out of words in the middle of the sentence. Gareth let it dangle until she found what she sought.

"Something you said, back on *Orgoth Vortai*," she continued, pausing again.

He continued with silence. He could remember every single one of those conversations, but had no idea what bit she might have latched onto.

"When you suddenly disappeared from the party," Diệu Ahn breathed slowly. "We had joked that you were a fashion writer with a secret identity, so you could get in places. Or a secret agent."

He let himself grow perfectly still.

That was exactly what they had talked about.

"When you left, you said *also* a secret agent, Gareth," her voice had fallen to a whisper. "Was that true?"

He took a deep breath. She would have found out eventually, if he wanted to cultivate her as a source. It was just his luck that she was also that smart, but he hadn't doubted that, having read more on the woman's background.

"It is," he said, just as quietly.

She paused.

He wondered if she was going to erupt in anger and throw him out. Or out him to the people he was trying to investigate.

"For who?" she finally asked quietly.

Gareth was still poised to throw himself to the side in case her hot chocolate was flying at his face, but she deserved an honest answer. At least as much of one as he could give.

"The Constabulary," he offered.

"Are you after me?" she asked in a small, frightened voice.

"Oh no, Diệu Ahn," he warmed, smiling at her in the low light. "My bosses consider you a good bet. Safe. They were hoping that you could innocently get us into some of the parties where the bad guys were."

"Like Gonquah?" she asked, her voice growing firmer, if not louder. "He's always been a bit of a scoundrel."

"Actually, this really was supposed to be a vacation for me," Gareth said. "Get to know you and meet some of your friends. Maybe spend some time being seen, so that later on, when I needed to be on a mission, I would be a face someone recognized, if we needed to do something, rather than a stranger off the street to be viewed suspiciously. Planting seeds now for fall harvesting."

"Something happened at the party last night," her voice turned in a new direction. "You reacted to the mechanical man in a strange way. Different from everyone else. Why was that?"

How much to tell her? Obviously, not much, or she would become terrified, and possibly turn on him anyway. But she would detect any falsehoods. He had so very little experience with lying, and women seemed to have a sixth sense for that sort of thing anyway.

"There are limits to what I can tell you," he

decided to go with some of the truth, and ruthlessly cut away the dangerous bits. "It wasn't the mechanical man, per se. It was the term that Gonquah used to describe it."

"*Android*, he called it," she repeated the term. "So fanciful. What does it mean?"

"Roughly, *in the shape of a man*, in an archaic, lost language nobody speaks anymore," Gareth shaded his truth carefully. "A female version would be a gynoid."

"What languages are forgotten, Gareth?" she was surprised. "This is the *Accord*. There is only the one language, that of the Chaa, plus some older dialects that are species-specific, and usually cultural terms, slang, to any one planet. Where does *android* come from?"

"I can't tell you, Diệu Ahn," Gareth replied. "And you are better off not knowing. But there is only one other person I am aware of in the entire *Accord* that would use that term, and he used it correctly to describe the mechanical man when talking to Gonquah. That machine is what I might also call an *Ellis Device*, after the first futurist that conceived of them in the modern context."

"He's your enemy, isn't he?" she asked, stepping past her confusion to lock onto his tones, perhaps, the anger that never left Gareth at what Marc had turned into. "That other."

Jealousy was a cruel taskmaster and a fickle mistress.

"That's right," Gareth nodded, even though it was almost too dark for him to see. "He is the man I have dedicated my life to stopping, primarily because he represents a threat to the entire *Accord of Souls*, if we fail."

"Do you need to leave again?" she asked, perhaps a little hurt. "To chase after him?"

"Actually, if I could, I would ask your help to get closer to Gonquah, so that we can find out more," Gareth replied. "To find that man, and stop Gonquah from helping him."

"Why is an android so dangerous, Gareth?" she leaned forward, voice sharp and insistent now. "Why is it a threat to the very *Accord*?"

"It is a tool, a device that can be programmed, Diệu Ahn," he said. "The men and women of the *Accord of Souls* are bound into a single psionic resonance that prevents violence and had held the peace between species for fifty thousand years."

"And?"

"This man can program those robots to kill without any pity or remorse," Gareth said. "He can conquer the *Accord* because he will be able to murder anyone who might try to stop him."

Her tiny gasp spoke volumes. But he had also read up on her life closer than perhaps anybody but her physician or her solicitor, so he knew where he might find safe ground with this woman.

"And you think you can stop him?" she finally asked, voice again tiny and frightened.

"I've got to try," Gareth whispered.

# SEEKER

ANEN STUDIED the young woman seated across the desk from her for cues, but she had never met a human, so she had no easy way to identify if it would work.

The youngster did make her feel old, but Fatima Darzi was already a veteran officer, a Senior Constable whose acting skills had made her invaluable as a deep cover agent in several previous investigations. She could literally become someone else, almost before your eyes.

But these were humans. And she dared not consult her resident experts on that dangerous species, lest she tip her hand to what might have to come next.

Fatima was a Grace. That was the only species that could come even remotely close enough to the human bioform to try to pass as one without extensive and possibly irreversible surgery that would take far longer than the available time.

Vanir were more structurally similar, but even a

short Vanir would be so much taller than a human as to stand out. Nari were the right height and build, but you would never get past all the fur, and without it, they would look even more strange.

So a Grace was going to have to walk into the lion's den alone.

At least there was a human culture the young woman could call upon in this instance to aid her disguise. Fatima wore a crimson outfit apparently tailored exactly like a Women's Auxiliary of Earth Force's Sky Patrol. Knee length flowing skirt, with a long tunic-style jacket over that and a gold edge on both. The top was double-breasted down the left side with a series of gold buttons and embroidering in a complicated diamond pattern connecting the buttons on both sides. It had a tall, folding collar, edged in gold like the rest of the tunic, with more embroidery on the cuffs. A black belt around her waist could hold a holster, according to the pictures Anen had seen, but Fatima would not need one.

Or rather, if she did, she would already be running for her life and need more help than a mere firearm would give her.

Fatima would pretend to be Persian, according to the notes. Anen had studied just enough of the background to understand the religious garb the young woman wore on her head today, a thing called a hijab. It was a long piece of cloth, almost a wide scarf, worn centered on the forehead and wrapped around and tucked in such that only the face was visible. And none of the woman's sensory tentacles.

Without them, Fatima did look human. It was rather eerie, staring at her, but the young agent just sat patiently and smiled back demurely.

"Tell me about the origins of the costume," Anen said suddenly, watching the woman for things that might give away her alien nature.

"Persia is an ancient land on Earth," Fatima said easily, adding an interesting accent to her tones, as though one who had learned another language growing up and transitioned later. "It has been a center for intellectual activity and scholarship going back to the late Bronze Age, for humans, but in modern times has remained something of a cultural backwater, far removed from the major centers of power in Earth Force."

"And the wrap on your head?" Anen asked.

"The religion of that region of Earth is called *Islam*," Fatima answered easily. "A follower is known as a Muslim, one who has submitted to their one God: Allah. A Muslim woman is supposed to dress conservatively, covering herself with modesty. Depending on the sub-culture, that might be as little as a hair scarf such as you might wear, or as much as something called a burqa, which completely engulfs the woman, except for her eyes. In some sects, even the eyes are then covered over with a mesh. All one might see are the hands. However, Persia sees itself as more open to educated and liberated women, within limits, so the hijab is generally sufficient. Among the English or the Americans of Sky Patrol, they will most likely not even know the term, but will immediately understand me as a foreigner, and a non-threatening one, so that will hopefully give me some level of flexibility to make cultural mistakes, being an obvious outsider. It will be a dangerous game we play with them, already."

"And your sensory tentacles?" Anen pressed.

"I have been working hard to keep them still," Fatima nodded. "Additionally, I will take certain drugs that will minimize movement, at a small cost to myself in terms of sensory input. As our Grace joke goes, I will become one of you instead."

They shared a smile. The Grace lived in such a rich sensory environment at all times that it was a wonder they only became artists, and not complete madmen.

"And you are prepared to escape?" Anen turned serious now.

"I have my transmitter, which will remain with me at all times," Fatima nodded, sobering. "It also has a dead-man capacity on my heartbeat, as well as triggering an alarm if I am separated from it by more than thirty meters. My backup team here has instructions to pull me out if that happens, on the theory that anything the humans see can be later discounted, if there is no body or evidence that an alien walked among them."

"You said body," Anen noted.

"These are humans, First Inspector," Fatima's voice was serious now as Anen listened to the underlying tones. The unsaid. "Not counting Dankworth, they are known to be dangerous and prone to unprovoked violence, even to their own kind. A true alien risks immediate death at their hands. In addition, we must penetrate to the heart of one of their most secure military facilities and discover what one of the most intelligent humans known has discovered."

"I do not like the idea of sending anyone on a suicide mission, Fatima," Anen said. "In this case, it is my hope that we can somehow find a lesser solution to the human problem. Even now, the High Commission is quietly discussing whether or not to simply wipe out the species, possibly with a biological weapon of some sort. Your mission is to give me other options. As humans are not part of our psionic pattern, it may be enough to kill this scientist, this Royston Loughty, and anyone else who could replicate his work."

"I understand, First Inspector," Fatima said.

"Find me a way to save as many people as you can," Anen ordered her.

"I will do what I can."

Anen hoped it would be sufficient. She had become a cop to protect and serve. But that wasn't supposed to be limited to only the *Accord*. What kind of officer was she if she couldn't protect those ignorant savages as well?

# ANOTHER MAN TAKEN

ROYSTON PROBABLY SHOULD HAVE WASHED his own mouth out with soap, due to the vile profanity that escaped when he first opened the report that had been compiled by the Women's Auxiliary Service. It didn't help that Pippa was seated close by in his office, reading Plutarch in the original Latin as a way to relax.

She merely looked up with one tart eyebrow raised at him, which caused Royston to blush all the more furiously.

No parent likes being caught being naughty by their own children, however grown and mature the latter.

She powered her reader down and set it primly on the edge of his desk with an expectant eye, the very image of innocence while still radiating a type of intellectual curiosity in his direction.

Without ever mentioning the profanity he had used.

Which made it worse. He had heard her use the same word previously.

"I had described the entire experiment in as particular detail as I was able," Royston explained to her. "And then trusted that most magical of quantities to pursue it."

"Oh?" she tilted her head just enough that he nearly laughed out loud. As if she could fool him.

"Woman's intuition," Royston supplied. "I told them what happened and asked if anyone else had ever disappeared thus. They went back and culled through the records, eliminating all the obvious false leads put out by people suffering some established levels of delusion or *Munchhausen By Proxy*. What was left was then rated in order of reliability, which was, in most cases, akin to asking how many angels could dance on the head of a pin."

"And what did those vile witches in the Records Department find for you, Father?" she batted her eyelashes at him, which did make him chuckle.

Until he glanced down at the folder in front of him.

"One incident, a little more than a year ago," he sobered instantly. She did the same, watching his face change. "The golden glow and unexplained disappearance were what whichever woman who did this keyed in on. And she found this one in the official records."

"Who?" Pippa asked, color draining out of her face.

"Marc Sarzynski," he supplied.

Rather than curse as he had, Pippa gasped, and her hands flew to her mouth. Not that she didn't know those words as well, but she was less likely to use them than he was, even in the privacy of his office.

After a moment, she calmed, resting her hands in her lap again.

"That would explain why Gareth then, Father," she offered. "As well as possibly the timing, if they needed him to go be a hero, as you suggested to the Queen."

"Yes, indeed," Royston nodded. "The man had disappeared entirely, right at the moment when Gareth had cornered his gang and was able to arrest the rest of them. I remember now, him mentioning their stories about a bizarre golden light, which at the time suggested that Marc had somehow used some unknown device to hypnotize those hard men into believing he had vanished, so they couldn't turn on him when he got away from them."

"But suppose he really did vanish?" Pippa asked. "What would that mean?"

"Perhaps, like Gareth, someone decided they needed a man like Marc," Royston suggested. "That might, in turn suggest why someone else would have chosen Gareth, in order to thwart him."

"So now we're reduced to suggesting the hosts of heaven and hell are girding themselves for some final battle?"

Her tone only mildly suggested the heavy weight of sarcasm behind it, but Royston had to shrug.

"Information insufficient, Daughter," he said. "I do not know how long the radiation residue might last that would at least confirm a level of similarity."

"No," she said peremptorily. "But you have built a detector for it."

"I have," Royston agreed.

"Perhaps we need to build warning devices," she said. "Like vacuum detectors, but warning about someone opening a wormhole such as you did. As the ancients like to say: *Once is chance. Twice coincidence. But three times is enemy action.* Are we perhaps suborned with enemy agents? Aliens able to hide in plain sight because we've never even considered their existence?"

"Or are we overreacting?" he countered. "Seeing patterns where none actually exist because we so desperately want to see it? Worse, will I become a laughingstock for suggesting it?"

"Don't tell them why," his daughter turned sharp. "Just build the thing, and leave a few around with instructions to contact you immediately if it goes off. Let them draw their own conclusions, as most people only understand that you have detected a new kind of radiation. Only the ones in the know will appreciate that it might be a portal warning."

"Yes, I believe that would be the most prudent course of action, Pippa," Royston agreed. "What would I do without you?"

"Get yourself into even worse situations than the ones you do now?" she smiled tartly and winked at him.

Royston smiled back, but underneath he felt the chill of death when he looked down at that report again while she went back to reading. There hadn't been a more dangerous criminal alive than Marc, once that man turned to evil and threw away his entire past. And did it because the young woman across from him had chosen Gareth instead.

If those two men were matching wits now in

some broader, alien galaxy, might it not risk being considered *Götterdämmerung*?

# INSIDE JOB

GARETH WAS EYE CANDY TODAY, and he knew it. Diệu Ahn had contacted Gonquah, or perhaps just knew the itinerary of the ongoing party around the man, so they had ended up at another event where Gonquah was. It wasn't one of that man's parties, like the one on his yacht, but had started off at a musical performance of a small mixed chorus before eventually ending up in the private wing of a casino.

Gareth had never seen many of the games being played, nor the card decks, so he was fascinated. Unlike the rectangular Hoyles of home, these were triangles as big as his palm, with about an inch cut off of the points to make them strange hexagons.

Gareth leaned nearby against one end of a bar, well away from the players at the big table centering the medium-sized room, as Diệu Ahn, Gonquah, and several other high rollers played for pots roughly equal to the annual salary of a shipping clerk in a major *Accord* corporation. He had a glass of something fruity and only mildly alcoholic to sip at, as well as a hexagonal plate with a variety of exotic dim sum piled up.

And several young women smiling at him from around the room, but he just smiled back and patiently ignored all of their attempts to flirt. Like a boy-toy that was attached to Diệu Ahn and unwilling to risk his meal ticket.

It was a weird place to live.

But it was obvious that this wasn't the first time the facility had hosted this sort of thing, and perhaps not even this group. There were bars on three walls, doing a brisk business in wines, spirits, and teas respectively. A kitchen was through a door on the fourth wall, with a staff back there apparently dedicated to this room alone, because no order took very long to be delivered.

Gareth enjoyed himself as he munched. People-watching had always been one of his hobbies, trying, as a cop did, to suss out everything he could about a random stranger just from the way they walked or dressed.

Most of the people in this room fell into one of three major categories, excluding the employees in black shirt, black pants, black aprons, and various species, or the managers in nice suits with white shirts and ties.

The fabulously rich were playing at the table. A dozen of them, roughly, with piles of chips in front of them done in that same cut-triangle hexagon as the cards, made in copper, silver, and gold colors. Some of those piles matched the annual revenue of medium-sized companies, relatively.

The next tier down were mostly people not quite as

fabulously wealthy, or perhaps not as addicted to the games of skill and personality that poker represented. If less wealthy, they dreamed of becoming big enough to get invited to play at this table. Others apparently had the wealth, but not the interest, so instead were people-watching like Gareth was.

The final tier were attached to one of the other groups. Gareth wasn't so prudish as to be offended that many of the men and women in here had Plus Ones that weren't their legal spouses. After all, that was the role he himself was playing, and at least a quarter of the big shots in here were female. Frequently the powerful men and women in here had what the vice teams back home had once taught Gareth to call boy-toys or rent-boys, depending on the gender combinations involved.

It was generally illegal on Earth, but many of the off-world colonies took a more libertine approach to those sorts of things. And Earth Force Sky Patrol didn't pass judgement, it just enforced the laws as they were in the jurisdiction asking for help. Crimes involved someone getting hurt physically or financially, not socially.

And he had a role to play, so he watched people watch people. It kept his mind and skills sharp.

A man approached Gareth as the game built to one of those massive pots where the egos of three people got personally involved. Diệu Ahn had presumably-wisely folded early, as she watched the men: a Nari, a Vanir, and Gonquah himself, began betting utterly ridiculous amounts of chips.

"Garrette?" the man asked as he sidle his massive bulk up and leaned against the bar, watching the spectacle innocently if you were far enough away to not hear anything.

"Gareth," he corrected the man, never looking over, even though he had never been this close to a Vratha before.

They reminded him of the massive pachyderms of earth, especially the semi-prehensile trunk that emerged from the center of the face and was nearly as long as a businessman's tie. The skin was heavy as well, rough and with that same sort of grayish tinge. Big ears on the sides weren't quite as semaphoric as a Nari's, but came close. The only big difference between a Vratha and a bipedal elephant was the crest of hair on the head and running most of the way down the back, rather like a horse. Other than that, the species had fine hair like a human covering most of their body.

"Ah," the man said. "I stand corrected. I understand you are a friend of Diệu Ahn's and she said you're a reporter?"

"I dabble," Gareth's tone suggested that anything like formal work was a stretch, and that perhaps he was more of a trust-fund child, as so many of the second tier in this room were.

You had to own something that generated an amazing cash flow to have enough wealth to play with the big kids.

"Oh?" the Vratha replied innocently. "My name is Aning Nocia."

Gareth smiled, but only on the inside, as the man's first name was pronounced exactly like awning and now Gareth would forever associate the man with umbrellas.

Nocia was perhaps six and a half feet tall, but

probably weighed as much as Gareth did, built more like a mobile tree trunk than anything else. Vratha women occasionally had some suggestion of hips and bust, but also tended to be mistaken for Ionic columns in nature.

"Gareth," he replied. "How can I be of assistance, Mr. Nocia?"

Keep it polite and simple. Gareth didn't have to impersonate the type of airhead that many of the men in here went for.

Diệu Ahn had played him off to strangers as an intellectual type, reminding folks around here that he was probably a secret agent art critic, a tale that people from that other party, like Gonquah, would no doubt be spreading as they started to outbid each other for miniature copies of Londra or other places from a woman who worked by hand over months.

"I'm something of an art collector, Gareth," the Vratha said in a low, friendly tone, speaking out of the side of his mouth like two strangers watching the horses and just happening to be leaned at the bar. "But I have a bit of a problem on my hands and wondered if I might bribe your expertise?"

Gareth was intrigued now, but kept things inside. Strangers, randomly met.

He was really watching Gonquah play a hand of poker for astronomical sums against two other men he assumed saw themselves as experts and mistook the Th'Tarni as a mark.

Gareth could have corrected their foolish assumptions, had they asked. He had watched Gonquah selling them rope earlier in the evening, but the tiny man was now in the process of setting the hook and reeling it in with just enough slack to draw them, rather than fighting.

You had to tire a swordfish out, not drag it kicking and screaming aboard the boat.

So Gareth glanced over at the Vratha man, rather than speak. It was a kind of side eye that suggested Gareth was listening, but not committing to anything.

"I have acquired a few paintings in my time," the man murmured, pausing to grab and take a gulp from a glass as a steward brought a tray around. "I've trusted my hunter in the past, but I'm beginning to wonder if he's in on a scam of some sort, passing off fake masters into private collections."

"I see," Gareth suggested a greater depth of knowledge on the field with his tone than he actually had, but he knew criminality probably better than most of the people in the room.

Probably not all of them, but he wasn't sure which few warranted greater vigilance.

Not yet, anyway.

"And you haven't asked a professional expert because...?" his words dangled. Setting that hook in the swordfish's mouth, as it were.

"Well," the man hemmed a bit. "Some of these pieces supposedly still hang in other collections. But I wonder if perhaps there weren't multiple copies made, and the original left alone."

"And how might I help, Mr. Nocia?" Gareth glanced over now, making eye contact to express some level of interest.

He found it terribly amusing that he might suddenly stumble into art fraud as a second

Constabulary career, if he managed to stay out of prison once Marc Sarzynski was stopped. Still, crime was crime. Stopping small time lawbreakers prevented them from growing up into major menaces at a later date.

And Diệu Ahn would probably giggle at the thought. As near as Prime Investigators on Almar had been able to determine, looking very closely, the woman didn't even have a parking ticket to her name. But she had inherited more money than even she knew what to do with, and employed experts to watch the experts watching her money. It helped that she knew accounting and signed her own checks for any amount larger than dinner.

And was smart enough to bail out of hands like this one playing out in front of everyone. It might be the end of the evening, as Gonquah had both men matching outrageous bets and running low on table stakes as the last hand of cards was dealt face down.

Nocia cleared his throat with a sound like a subway passing underneath the streets of New Metropolis. Low and subsonic, deep in your bones.

"Might I host you two at my palace sometime soon?" he asked diffidently. "Perhaps show you a few things in a more private setting and get your opinions?"

Gareth let a smile form briefly before returning to the neutral look as the tension built over there. The rest of the room was so riveted on the card play that he might have been able to rob one of the bartenders and get into a shootout with another one and not have anybody notice.

"I understand that my dance card might be

booked up for a bit," Gareth murmured back to the man. "But you can ask her and I won't object."

"Thank you," the man Gareth thought of as an umbrella nodded and made his way quickly off as Gonquah turned over his last card to cheers as well as cries of anguish and disgust.

That was not a man you should ever bet against. Unless you knew what cards he was holding.

INTRUDER


THE NIGHT WAS dark and calm. Perfect hunting weather for something like this.

Marc's team was in an alleyway near the delivery gate of a small, urban estate.

Watching.

For Marc, the best part of all the training this last summer had been watching his people move to a level of professionalism almost on a par with the sorts of gangsters he had been able to take for granted back home. Lots of *Accord* citizens were broken to one degree or another, he had found, but few had the capability to do intentional violence to one another.

Finding such people had been like sifting hay for needles. Or diamonds in a coal mine. But he had succeeded. In addition to the original trio he had kept, Mishalska's anger at being bested by the android had broken something in the youngster.

It gave him an odd symmetry on the team, as Marc watched them prepare. Two Warreth females, barely out of their teenage years, and two Nari men, one older and scientific and the other a young Turk who had taken Marc's advice and let his fur grow back out to a single length.

Never leave the cops a visual identifier when they go back and review the tapes of an event.

Not that there would be much the tapes would be able to show that didn't just confirm everything the cops already suspected, but they should be in the habit of not making it easy. Everyone was dressed in baggy black clothes that would hide identities, if not races.

After all, a Vanir male, two Warreth females, and several Nari males committing crime was going to identify him to Gareth and those other two Constables without any doubt. Assuming that they could do anything about it. It didn't matter what they thought of the sixth figure, dressed for now like another Nari.

Marc had spotted the standard cameras in the obvious places. Effective enough to deter amateur criminals, but this particular model didn't even come equipped with microphones to record ambient sound. There were probably a few other units he had missed, but these people simply had no understanding of violence as a tool, or crime as something to be solved later by experts with as much information as possible.

Amateurs.

"Android," he quietly addressed the machine dressed as a person. "Are you ready?"

"This unit is prepared," the machine answered back, drawing two pistols from shoulder holsters and holding them out for inspection. "The disintegrator and the stunner are fully charged and have been tuned to acceptable levels of accuracy."

"Very good," Marc said. "Stand by for action."

"Standing by," it said.

Marc turned to the others. Maiair and Yooyar held disintegrators, while the Nari had stunners. Like the machine, Marc had one of each in thigh holsters, where he could get at them quickly, but for now would rely on size, speed, and wits.

"Zorge, Mishalska, shoot anything that moves inside. Am I clear?" he asked them, towering like a redwood above the shorter men.

Both nodded. Mishalska might have gulped, but this would be his baptism by fire. The others had been there with him before at least once.

Marc turned to the women.

"The boys are out front," Marc reminded them. "You are responsible for doors and things that a stunner will not affect."

Maiair nodded. Yooyar grinned with her head crest and eyes.

Marc moved out of the deeper darkness to the gate and tested the handle with a gloved hand. Locked, but he knew that. Getting it unlocked would either require someone inside hitting a button, or someone outside spending a lot of time fiddling with electronics.

Marc preferred a more direct approach.

"Android, destroy the lock and open the gate," he ordered quietly, stepping to one side to watch.

The Ellis Device raised its left hand and fired. There was a small popping noise as metal sublimed under an intense explosion of sudden heat. The machine stepped forward and hipchecked the gate out of the way, scanning the interior courtyard with careful eyes. He shot two other cameras a quickly as he could process their locations and cycle the weapon.

One of the reasons Marc had been willing to try this place was the lack of outside guard dogs. Not that he had anything about shooting dogs, but they would make a lot of noise and might wake neighbors at the wrong moment.

The backyard was empty. A nice patio for hosting small parties. A pool and hot tub for summer fun. Old trees and a small garden for kitchen herbs. It had a very homey feel.

Marc wondered if the current owners would eventually sell the place rather than live with the memories of what had happened tonight.

Marc led his ragged convoy of killers across the piazza quickly and approached a rear door to the garage. The android reached out and shot something even as Marc spotted the small camera above the door.

There was a small hole there now. About big enough for a chipmunk to take up residence later, if this planet had an equivalent creature like that.

The second shot went into the door, annihilating a portion of the sill and the strike plate in a quick flash of light. Just like he had laid it out for the machine earlier.

Inside, the garage had just enough night lights on to see the door to the house. This one was heavier, fireproofed against events in the garage.

"Hinges," Marc ordered quietly.

The machine shot the right hand frame in three places, bursting quick holes in the pseudo-wood and revealing the destroyed hinges holding it upright.

"Remove the door quietly and set it to one side," Marc ordered.

He would have done it, but even with gloves on the immense heat would scorch his hands.

The android holstered both pistols and grabbed handle and middle gap. It pushed forward and Marc was sure he heard metal tearing inside the door itself. He drew his own stun pistol now and watched the widening gap as the android stepped into the kitchen and pivoted to lean the door against a wall.

There were no dogs present. Or, they weren't fed and watered in the kitchen, which was what he would have expected. Thus far good.

The android drew his sixguns again and took the lead. The kitchen and dining room were empty. The salon and entryway as well.

Nobody in the library or the downstairs bathrooms.

The last little hallway led to the laundry room, and the first risk on this venture. They moved like ghosts, another benefit of six months training in the desert. There. A door tucked in behind the pantry.

"Destroy the lock and stun the inhabitant," Marc whispered.

He presumed the *au pair* would have a locking door, just in case the father got drunk and decided to make a pass at a teenage girl. He had heard rumors about the gentleman. It was one of the reasons this house had been chosen, rather than one of the others. People who were already crooked were easier to bend.

The android studied the situation for a moment,

and then moved so quickly that it was probably a blur to everyone else. But they weren't used to high-speed mayhem. The lock shattered with a hard kick, the door swung open but the android caught it with the barrel of the disintegrator before it could slam into the wall.

On the bed, a young Grace girl slept. Marc guessed she was barely eighteen, only because that was the legal minimum age for a job like this.

Eyes opened, but the android shot her before she managed to come fully awake. Hopefully, this would be nothing but a bad dream she would forget on waking. There was nothing a teenage Grace girl could have done to stop him tonight.

Best she not be hurt trying.

Marc moved to the bottom of the stairs and scanned the balcony above. This space showed fantastic wealth. Old money that had been collecting items for a long time and putting them to best show.

He turned to Maiair and Zorge.

"You two watch front and rear from downstairs," he ordered quietly. "We'll clear the upstairs."

Both nodded silently and moved: Zorge to the kitchen to cover their retreat, Maiair to the front door, in case someone had called the cops and a badge might come knocking, even at this time of night.

Up the stairs, noting that they were almost too small for Vanir, but that made sense. The owners were Traakna, and their shorter legs wouldn't appreciate a house that would make Marc comfortable.

The killer robot led, with Marc in its shadow. At the top, Marc pointed to Yooyar and indicated she should watch their rear, the far end of the hallway that faced a closed double-door right now.

First door revealed a bathroom, empty though showing indications of a youngster living here, with various bath toys piled haphazardly in a blue, plastic laundry basket. Cute, mermaid nightlight over the sink.

Back out into the hallway. Door open halfway into a room with lots of nightlights.

The android peeked in and rotated its head like an owl to look back at Marc.

"Female juvenile Traakna, master," it said in a quiet, mechanical voice.

Marc nodded and stepped around the machine man.

The Traakna girl, little Ariela, indeed slept, sprawled on a double bed in the middle of the room, surrounded by toys and decorations that made the place look like a fairy tale castle owned by unicorns. Her antennae twitched to some inner rhythm as she dreamed.

Marc studied the room quickly, identifying several targets before he aimed his own stun pistol and shot the child while she slept. He had specifically tuned his weapon down to for the task. Had the android done it, the weapon might have risked permanently damaging the child. An adult would be out cold for mere minutes if Marc shot them with his. That would still be enough for this group.

Marc knew himself to be a cold, evil man, but making war on innocent children was absolutely a bridge too far, even for him. She would sleep peacefully, and awaken in a new place with strangers, so Marc needed to identify the toys to bring along with them to keep her mollified for the few days or week he would need to keep her.

He turned to Mishalska and the robot. The Nari was showing a little too much white around his eyes, but Marc wasn't about to tease the man. Anybody who would hurt children for no reason had no place in his gang.

It was good.

They checked the library. A full office showed all manner of locked file cabinets Marc might have found interesting, but he simply didn't have the time. Another bathroom, this one decorated for company. An upstairs reading room that reminded Marc of the private chapels some old castles had maintained, but with only one bookcase, overflowing, and two plush chairs that looked like they were for midgets. Or Traakna.

The double-door at the end of the hall had remained closed when they joined Yooyar again. Marc gestured the others to move a little closer and tested the handle.

Unlocked.

He drew his pistol again and turned to the robot.

"Take the male and render him unconscious," Marc ordered. "I will stun the female."

"Acknowledged, master," the machine said.

Marc turned the knob and pushed quietly unsure what he would encounter.

The four of them spilled into a sitting room, large and comfortable and opening onto a balcony through closed, glass doors that admitted just enough moonlight to make the place cozy. An open door showed the sleeping quarters beyond, so Marc led them quickly to that door and peeked in.

There.

Elgannohn Shevskara and his wife, comfortably asleep.

Traakna reminded Marc of Yuudixtl, to some degree. At least in the sense that both had evolved from marine lizards, much like humans and Vanir had both started their evolutionary conquest as arboreal tree shrews.

Traakna had the bright green scales of a gecko, with a reverse-hinged legs like a dog or chicken and a long, almost prehensile tail. Two sensory antennae grew backwards out of the sides of their foreheads like gazelle horns. Big, expressive eyes were wider set than on most *Accord* species, giving them a tremendous peripheral vision. Nostrils and ears were just slits, and the mouth had almost no lips. Just a long, shockingly-pink tongue almost as prehensile as the tail.

The wife stirred in her dream, but Marc was shooting her anyway. The machine shot the husband almost as quickly.

"Check the room," Marc said unnecessarily.

Yooyar and Mishalska were already investigating the massive bathroom and his and hers walk-in closets.

"Clear," Yooyar announced a few moments later.

Marc nodded. He hadn't expected any troubles so far. Shevskara was a businessman, not troublemaker. And he would be even less so with a hostage involved.

"Android, carry the male," Marc ordered. "Mishalska, grab him some clothes to wear. Yooyar, with me."

Marc strode quickly back down the hall with the lethal Warreth woman in his wake.

He paused at the doorway to Ariela's bedroom, but she was out cold still. Good.

Marc moved quickly to grab a bag and stuff clothes and toys into it. A plush doll from the bed that reminded Marc of a sasquatch went into the bag, as well as a collection of unicorns and a few other things.

Yooyar watched from the door.

"Books," she said aloud.

Marc cast an interested eye in her direction. She was among the least-maternal females he had ever known, but she was still a woman. He grabbed several books off a nearby shelf and stuffed them into the bag, along with a twirly skirt hanging over a chair.

The bag went to Yooyar to carry.

Carefully, he picked up Ariela and wrapped her in a blanket. She was so small, relative to his new, massive size, that it was almost like holding an infant, even if the girl was the developmental equivalent of a six-year-old human.

He returned to the master bedroom and surveyed it, pulling an envelope from an inside pocket and resting it on the bed where Elgannohn had been sleeping and turned to leave.

"Just like that?" Yooyar asked. "It's really that simple?"

Marc smiled at her like a crocodile.

"Yes," he replied simply. "Kidnapping for profit is a time-honored way to make money, if you get a reputation for both ruthlessness and respectability in the process. And we will. I just need to train you how to handle it. And who to hunt."

"And Shevskara?" Yooyar asked as she followed him out the door and down the grand staircase.

"Something like this doesn't work nearly as well on an honest man, Yooyar," Marc said over his shoulder, tenderly watching that his bundle was safe. "But Shevskara can't even spell truthful."

Out the back, across the yard, and into the alley. Mishalska and the android had already tied the Traakna into a seat in the back of a passenger van, with Zorge in the driver's seat just waiting.

Ariela went into a child seat and got buckled fussily in. She would be returned to her mother in just a matter of days, regardless. Her purpose now was to get her father's undivided attention while Marc held the man captive. After that, knowing Shevskara, the man would be happy to buy his freedom as well.

"What was in the letter?" Yooyar asked as they pulled away.

"I have your daughter and your husband," Marc quoted it from memory. "You will follow my instructions to the letter. If you do not call the authorities, you will get Ariela back in a few days, after which we will discuss the ransom for your husband. We will be in touch."

"And humans do this thing for sport?" her face was scrunched up.

"Our reputation for ferocity with your kind is well deserved, Yooyar," he turned and smiled at her. "Here, it lets me do things that your kind can't even fathom, for the most part."

"And we're returning the child without getting

anything for it?" Yooyar followed up. It was obvious she was learning, not questioning.

"We're buying silence and collaboration," Marc said. "The wife will remain quiet. Elgannohn will be much less likely to be obstinate when I show the man that I have his only child in my possession. And then he will convince his wife to give us a significant amount of money, which will help fund the organization for a long while. If all goes according to plan, we will return him unharmed in a couple of weeks."

"And if they refuse?" Maiair asked from the front seat.

"They she gets her husband back in pieces."

# LIONS

FATIMA FELT ALMOST BLIND, walking out of the Arizona sun and into the transportation center in her disguise, dressed as a Woman's Auxiliary and carrying a bag with spare uniforms and such.

At least she could barely smell the bizarre human scents wafting about her as she got inside and away from the dry desert heat, but at the same time, she had to rely on her eyes for nearly everything.

No wonder the rest of the *Accord*, and perhaps the rest of the galaxy was so mundane. Everything with them was limited to a two-dimensional perception field that left out so many things.

But she was as prepared as she could be in the time given to assimilate. She had pills she could take that would help her process and absorb nutrients and vitamins from human food, and keep much of it from poisoning her in the process.

It helped that Earth Force Sky Patrol cuisine tended to be extremely bland, based largely on American or English cooking, which gravitated towards well-cooked meat, possibly in a mild sauce, with grilled or boiled vegetables on the side. This would be so much more of a dangerous adventure, if the standard was Javanese, or Pekinese, or perhaps Ecuadorian.

Stew she could handle.

And the clothing was outrageous, but again, she understood the bizarre cultural underpinnings that drove it. Males had returned to a peak of utter cultural dominance over the last few centuries, after reaching near parity at a previous juncture. Females of most cultures were relegated to a socially-subjugated state, expected to serve a man, defer to him, even cook for him upon marriage.

Just one more reason why this species was unfit for galactic civilization.

But she wasn't here to be a fashion critic. And the skirt she was forced to wear in public wasn't all that bad, as it had been specifically cut to give her a little more freedom to move than it should, and to moderate her temperature, depending on the situation and location. Even her brassieres had labels suggesting it came from a human factory, but someone had taken the time to fit them to her so that she would be comfortable in them, when the placement of her breasts was apparently closer together on her chest than most human females.

She had several identical uniforms, in gradually heavier weights of fabric, from the lightest silk for equatorial heat to a heavy wool gathered from a true Merino sheep on this very planet. In the field, she would be expected to add a prim, scarlet kepi matching the rest of her clothes, with a gold band, but that was inappropriate on a station or ship, as she would be boarding shortly.

Each uniform had been vacuum-sealed according to the Earth Force Sky Patrol regulations she had studied, to be as flat as possible and then packed into a carryall, along with personal items and an electronic reader with a variety of human-entertainment options and books programmed into it, in case she wanted to learn more about some of the more interesting bits of the amazing number of cultures on this single planet. And boredom was likely to be her biggest risk, if everything else went well.

English words on a monitor as she entered the hallway directed her to a smaller corridor on her left, away from the larger mass of humans in the process of moving to her right into the larger facility. Down a short hallway tiled in white or black rectangles and through a door, Fatima found herself in what she guessed was a small waiting room, with a woman seated behind a counter, wearing the identical uniform to hers.

"May I help you?" the person asked brightly. Guard, security, or official wasn't readily obvious from the arrangement of things, but Fatima suspected that to be an intentional thing.

She took a quiet breath and approached the counter, reaching inside her tunic to withdraw a set of papers that she placed on the counter.

"I have orders to report here for transport," Fatima said simply. Perhaps adding a level of confusion to her voice as misdirection.

Certainly, she wasn't entirely sure of this process. She would be writing up most of the infiltration manual for future female agents, if she was successful.

And if humans were still an ongoing concern in another year.

The official pulled the stack of papers apart and sorted them. Passport. Sky Patrol Identity Card. Orders To Report.

Fatima rocked back into her heels and crossed her hands behind her, a close enough approximation of the at-ease posture she had never learned in Earth Force Basic Training.

"Fatima Darzi?" the woman asked. "Persian physicist on detached duty?"

"That's right," Fatima nodded.

*Leave it at that. I am on a secret mission for Sky Patrol and you do not have the security clearance to even know who I am, let alone why I am here.*

The woman nodded in turn and began typing into a computer hidden on the other side of the tall desk.

Fatima measured the steps to the door, if she should have to run. And if the door wasn't locked by the time she reached it.

Humans relied extensively on computer networks for information, which was bad, but they also didn't trust them, so the systems were not highly automated, nor efficient, settling on massive redundancy instead. And they were greatly fragmented, with no organization trusting any other to host critical data or information.

As a result, it made their information security a nightmare to penetrate, but only because you had to do the same job twelve times, rather than just changing one setting and letting it ripple out through the rest of the electronic forest.

And it took time. But it also took time to look something up, and to cross-reference it, if necessary. And something missing from another system might merely mean that you didn't have the clearance to see it there, or maybe it hadn't been typed in already.

Primitives who have only just barely begun to look on information as a tool, rather than a weapon.

Fatima managed not to goggle in surprise when the woman opened her passport and stamped it with a mechanical device made from chrome. One that left ink on the page.

How utterly antiquated. And easy to fake later.

"Here you are," the woman said with a smile. "I've checked you in for the flight already and assigned you a window seat. The kitchen is prepared for a halal meal. Right through there."

She handed everything back and Fatima stuffed it back into the inner pocket of her tunic, on her hip under the flap, rather than higher, across her breasts.

Fatima wondered if having the pocket higher up on her chest where it would be more comfortable was forbidden. Where perhaps something in the pocket might alter the shape of the breast so much, or cover it, that male commanders had vetoed it at some previous juncture. Sexism run out of control. Men had such a pocket and didn't give it a second thought.

Still, she kept her opinion to herself as she circled the counter and approached a door. It buzzed loudly at a signal from behind the desk and she pulled it open, emerging into a much nicer lounge.

Red carpeting with a thick shag. Soft blue walls.

Floor to vaulted ceiling windows looked out over one of North America's southern skyports. Comfortable chairs. Even a refrigerator with a transparent front and filled with bottles of various kinds.

She retrieved a glass bottle of orange juice and grabbed a bag of salted nuts from a nearby bowl before retreating to one of the seats and relaxing. Even the smells were better in here. Less industrial cleaner and perhaps more floral orange and rose. It at least smelled natural, in her greatly-reduced olfactory state. Her tentacles probably could have measured the exact chemical signature to a degree that she could either identify the source chemicals, or tell when the flowers had been cut and then infused into an alcohol base for dispersion.

It was still so much better to not have to deal with the smells of the humans in here.

None were close to her, but she was being covertly watched by several. Two Anglo men in Earth Force uniforms looked like middle-aged managers returning from a business conference. A pair of East Asian women in Women's Auxiliary uniforms similar to hers. An African-looking male in a Sky Patrol Field Agent uniform confused her for a second, because she hadn't emotionally prepared herself for the fact that humans occasionally got large enough that they might pass for Vanir with a little work.

She kept thinking of them as being at her scale, and yet just the human diversity in this lounge put paid to that. Interesting. It had been an academic exercise before, as white Anglos were so dominant in Sky Patrol, and shared responsibilities with the teeming masses of East Asia and South Asia inside Earth Force itself.

Fortunately, her hijab served the secondary purpose of marking her out as a stranger. Persia was a member of Earth Force, but rarely contributed forces to Sky Patrol, as they had almost no off-world colonists. Further west from Fatima's supposed homeland, the folks of the Levant had perhaps taken up that slack, being over-represented both in Sky Patrol and among the merchants and traders of deep space.

So the various people in the lounge left her alone, except for a brief, commiserative smile from the African male she suspected was meant to convey a comradeship over being outsiders here. She lacked the genetic background to automatically make sense of human mannerisms that apparently transcended culture.

By the time the juice and nuts were gone and being slowly processed in her system for useful nutrients, another woman had joined them from the hallway behind her, and several men from a different doorway. They were all Earth Force, but not Sky Patrol, so apparently the flight today was a mostly-civilian sort of thing, and not a military transport.

A woman appeared from a third door at one side and spoke into a microphone that projected her words cleanly across the giant lounge.

"Good afternoon, ladies and gentlemen," she said professionally. "Flight *Arizona-Seven* to Earth Force Headquarters at the L1 LaGrange point, with subsequent service to The Arsenal at L2 is now ready to load. Please have your ID and orders ready and we will board the bus to take us across the field."

Fatima joined the group lining up, and found herself behind the East Asian women and just in front of the African man. She could feel almost at home, if she pretended they were Nari and he was Vanir.

The bus was a large box with comfortable seats, riding on vulcanized rubber tires and powered by batteries. She had a fantastic view as they crossed the landing field, watching sub-orbitals, ballistics, and simple airliners moving about in a complicated dance.

Again, so strange, when she was used to flying auto-taxis that would take you to a tube station, from which you would simply transit a wormhole to a second location, or jump up to orbit and board a liner making a set run of stops, like an enormous space freighter.

*Arizona-Seven* was a small, winged aircraft, located at the farthest end of the field. A white tube lying flat, with portholes to see out of, and a tall fin like a predatory fish at the rear. Four large engines made up the stern of the craft, currently being fueled by a pair of tanker trucks.

Fatima was indeed in a window seat. The flight was small enough that she had nobody in the aisle seat next to her, but she couldn't be sure if that was luck, or if the agent at the desk had decided to isolate her from the others, lest her strange, Persian ancestry infect them.

Little did they know.

She grinned to herself and set to connecting all the appropriate straps and buckles.

The seat was deep and comfortable. The safety briefing far more complex and detailed than any back home, but her culture also had been flying in space since before this species discovered metals. Fatima worked to calm herself that the speech was to cover multiple eventualities, rather than representing probabilities.

Was it really likely that they would face a water landing? Possibly, given that the planet itself had just a large water surface ratio, and so much land was farther away from their equatorial flight path.

It was mind-numbingly loud when the engines ignited. She was so happy to be nearly deaf already, without her tentacles. She could only imagine the migraine that so much noise might trigger.

The Arizona desert was flat and brown as the craft lifted off and began to climb to a much higher elevation. Eventually, the air would thin and the wings would retract to just stubs as they relied more and more on the roaring thrust behind her.

It took hours just to reach orbit, and the better part of a day to reach the gravitationally-stable high ground over the planet/moon system. She slept through some of it, relaxing in the absence of gravity. Two meals were eaten that were neither here nor there, and she spent the rest of her time reading current news from various sources on the planet below, and the stations ahead. Humans being humans, which was to say dangerous monsters, but they did appear to be trying to better themselves, once they managed to not hate each other over differences in color, shape, size, or religion. At least according to some of the news she read.

Fatima didn't have a lot of hope for most of them, but the First Inspector had sent her here to try to find a way to save the species, in spite of themselves. She could do that. Earth Force and Sky Patrol did represent an attempt to unify the humans into a better whole, however pale a shadow of the *Accord* it was at present.

Perhaps someday the Chaa would find a way to integrate these people as well.

The business managers and most of the females debarked when the vessel docked at Sky Patrol Headquarters, with a number of Sky Patrol officers and staff boarding in their place. This next flight was more crowded, but she was still did not have anyone in the seat next to her to bother her during her meals and sleep patterns, so she presumed a level of discrimination by that first woman, as other females on the two flights had been seated with males. Only the Muslim was kept isolated.

Good to know, and useful to her disguise.

*Arizona-Seven* was close to her destination before she finally caught a glimpse out her porthole, of the place called alternatively *The Arsenal* and *Shadow Base One*, for its location at the L2 LaGrange point, the so-called *Far Side of the Moon* from the system's sun, having run a slingshot from the inner point to the outer.

The base itself was a huge, spinning cylinder seen edge on, like a hollow tube just about than four kilometers across with massive spokes running from the central axis column out to the living quarters around the inner edge. She was looking forward to being back in pseudo-gravity again, after several days in free-fall. Again, primitives that had only just managed to make it into space on the backs of basic physics, and nothing more advanced.

And hopefully she could help to keep it that way.

*Arizona-Seven* docked to one end of the hub and she debarked with the others, floating out to the edges of a small chamber under the watchful eyes of several, male, Sky Patrol officers who reminded her of nothing so much as mother ducks with happy ducklings intent on meandering about.

Into a small elevator, where each of them was seated into a quick harness and inspected, before this platform was sent on its ways, with gravity going from a suggestion to a force as they descended outward to the edges of the station.

Inside, one more quick check of her paperwork and orders, and she was assigned to an unwed females barracks, with her own private room and shower attached to a communal eating and study facility. She unpacked her various uniforms and stowed them into a closet, set out her items supposedly issued by a quartermaster back in Tehran, and then settled herself on the bed to meditate.

She had entered the lion's den. Shortly, she would have to meet the lion himself.

## UNDERCOVER

HIS INSTRUCTIONS HAD BEEN SUCCINCT, detailed, and a little strange, but Gareth had assumed they were the product of years or perhaps decades of deep-cover experience that he didn't have. Heck, until this, he had never had any interest in even becoming an undercover agent. Of course, if his secret got out to the general public, that would no longer be an option.

Unless Talyarkinash could somehow transform him again and not kill him in the process.

It was weird being the only person around who could dream of becoming someone else. Well, not counting Marc, and Gareth wasn't. After so many years as that man's friend, he couldn't see Marc radically changing his appearance. Even the new ears and the altered shape of his skull to make him Vanir was probably as jarring in his mirror as it was Gareth's. Marc wouldn't go any further visibly. Probably just stronger and faster if he could.

The joint Gareth had entered was what he would

have called a truck stop, back home. Located out on the edge of town, he had taken an auto-taxi, jumped clear over to *Datha*, which was one of the newer worlds in the *Accord*, then followed the directions.

This place was nobody's homeworld, so it was an interesting mix of Yuudixtl, Vanir, and Nari, already three of the most common species in the *Accord*, along with Enjev, Moisa, and a fairly significant group of Tree People.

Gareth grinned to himself as he walked in, contemplating that a tribe of Tree People, or Quarrie as they were more properly known, really was called a Forest. There weren't any in here, but a group was standing in a nearby clearing, probably absorbing sunlight and dew for breakfast.

The restaurant itself was about as divie as he could have imagined. Booths down both sides with tables in the open middle. The dominant table coloration was a polished cherry oak, with black leather, so it was rather darker than most of the ones he had known as a kid or young agent, where white was the main color. A counter stuck out into the middle like a horseshoe, and a window behind it showed the kitchen.

Gareth was dressed down today. Back from his nicer duds to dungarees and his denim jacket. It fit in well with the midafternoon crowd as he looked around.

Baker was in the last booth on the right, opposite the bathrooms located on the left side of the counter. Gareth walked over and sat with his back to the room, but he wasn't too concerned about someone sneaking up on her.

"I got your message," she said, sipping some

coffee from an ugly, green mug. "What needed to be discussed in person?"

"I have a lead on Maximus," Gareth said quietly. "Or rather, someone that Maximus has possibly hired to make him weapons. Rather than just arrest our target in a big, public event that warns Maximus, I would like to break into the man's facility and gather up more evidence first."

"Why?" her eyes bored in on his like a laser cannon.

"Because what I have won't stand up in front of a grand jury, Baker," Gareth grimaced.

He explained the series of parties to her as they ordered and ate, including the reference to the Ellis Device that Gonquah had called by the English name: *Android*. The implications didn't register with her any more than they had with Diệu Ahn, but they were all *Bound*.

Only he could envision an army of killer robots turned loose on the general populace of the *Accord*, which was exactly what he feared might happen if they waited too long.

"Killer robots?" she still sounded dismissive.

"Think of them as guns with legs, then, Baker," Gareth snapped, still trying to keep his voice down as the waiter approached to clear plates and refill coffee. "They are about as controlled, considering the circumstances."

"This might be enough," she suggested after the they were alone again. "We could take it up the chain of command and get an opinion."

"You do that," Gareth said. "Or better yet, have Grodray. But in the meantime, I don't think any laws have actually been broken, other than providing goods and services to a known criminal, and I'm sure there are enough layers of obfuscation involved that he's safe there as well if his lawyers are any good."

"Gonquah has been on our list for a while, Gareth," she admitted finally. "As you surmised, nothing could be made to stick, but that's not the same as we haven't been trying. How would you build a killer robot?"

"The word he used was *android*," Gareth replied, his voice staying low and quiet as the restaurant's clientele came and went. "That suggests a bipedal silhouette, like a human or a Vanir, but I would make it roughly Nari sized to blend in better with the general public. All the usual sensors on the head, like a uhm…like one of me. Hands as well, with opposable thumbs, following the standard model. The only point at which you start breaking laws then becomes the moment you hand the thing a pistol and tell it to kill people."

"And they would not be programmed against such an occurrence?" she asked.

"You already have automation and robots in your factories, Baker," he said. "Immobile and massive and stupid. That's one of the reasons we invented the term android. To distinguish a special kind of machine. And Sarzynski isn't about to have them custom built for him with the standards Laws of Robotics baked in."

"Laws of Robotics?" Baker's face scrunched in confusion.

"A set of programming imperatives," Gareth said. "No robot can harm a human. Robots must follow all orders given them by humans, except when it would hurt a humans. Etc. They can get quite detailed, according to the Ethical Technologists who taught me at school. Those won't exist here."

"Okay," she finally nodded. "I'm convinced. You have really good instincts at this sort of thing. What do you propose?"

Gareth blushed at the compliment. This wasn't the hardass Constable he had known for so long. Perhaps having her prize in sight had made her a little less antagonistic all the time?

Or maybe people were finally valuing her like they should. Eveth Baker was one of the best cops Gareth had ever met. She deserved to be a peer of Grodray and the other Prime Investigators.

"I want to break in during the middle of the night," Gareth said. "Gonquah mentioned which factory had made the one in his suite, that first night when he told someone that they weren't ready for everyone to order yet, as they worked out the final specs and tested some in the field."

"Was he telling the truth?" Baker leaned forward abruptly. "Not ready yet?"

"Maybe," Gareth suggested. "It might also be that he didn't want others to have a chance to figure out what they were capable of. And if it were up to me, thinking like Maximus, I'd order a few and then find someplace very remote and quiet to push them as hard as I could to find their exact limits in the process of breaking them. Then come back and order a second batch with improvements and refinements."

"Does Earth have such armies?" Baker's eyes were showing white now.

"No," Gareth tried to satisfy her. "There was a stretch a few centuries ago where they did, and the violence and warfare got so far out of hand that a global government had to be formed to stop it and then prevent future wars. That's Earth Force. Sky Patrol are the cops that deal with criminals who want to break loose and return to those terrible days. But there are also groups that will come in and crush anyone trying to start a rebellion against the peace."

"So you think you'll just waltz in there by yourself and find what you need?" Baker's voice had a sharper note now.

Gareth nodded, unwilling to give her more details, as he would be most likely faking it every step of the way.

"No," Baker decided.

"No?" Gareth was shocked.

"No," she repeated. "You're not going in there by yourself and risk it."

"Why not?" Gareth asked.

Her sudden smile was almost more frightening than Eveth Baker angry.

"I'm coming with you."

# DEFENSIVE MEASURES

ROYSTON WAS confident enough in the design of the machine that he didn't need to go back through the entire, convoluted process of opening a new wormhole, down in Arizona, just to confirm that this detection device worked. His older machines had registered the sudden appearance of this new type of radiation in a concentrated form, and his original sensor worked well enough, when he went into Gareth's abandoned and sealed off cabin to test it.

The radiation itself was fading at a slow but measurable rate. Royston estimated it had a half-life of roughly eighty-three days, so he knew it would be too faint to detect in another year, swallowed back up into the cosmic background radiation it seemed to have been derived from in the first place.

Royston's lab was, as always, the dark mirror reflection of his office. Perfectly clean, as though a movie set put into storage, with every tool put away into a labeled slot in a drawer, clean and polished.

Nothing at all on the countertops themselves that wasn't there all the time. As opposed to his office, where books, papers, and old coffee mugs frequently competed with one another for space.

The two newest detectors waited patiently on a work counter, quiescent and poised, but Royston hadn't opened any portals in here. Nor, as far as he could tell, had anyone else. One device was small, a pocket-sized case no larger than necessary for holding cigarettes had an effective detection range of only a few meters, while the larger one was more the size of a desk phone, or perhaps a cigar box, and would both detect and then triangulate to a range of sixty or eight meters, depending on the materials blocking the signal. Neither had found anything new.

Hopefully, that situation would remain thus. He had woken from more than one nightmare fearing that his hypothetical aliens had learned of his new discoveries and were in the process of returning, in order to do something about it.

Something ugly.

He had no way to preventing a portal from being opened, if they wanted to just chuck a bomb through and destroy The Arsenal. That was one of the reasons that information about the generator he had built, including the fact that it had even worked, was so tightly controlled.

Someone else could teleport a bomb anywhere they wanted, if they took a fancy to the notion. And then the wars would return.

Royston made a mental note to take a week off, preferably with Pippa, and see if they could locate that one singer and her rock band. He hoped it would give him another chance at the sort of inspiration that had led him to this new mathematics in the first place. He could not imagine that the physics of the universe were not so well balanced that it was impossible to build a device to disrupt such a wormhole from forming.

He just needed to find them.

The outer door opened and Sector Marshal Siddall stepped through. The last few months had aged him badly. Royston had known Alvin for more than twenty years, and in that time, the now-Head of The Arsenal had always been a tall, heavy-set man. Over the last few years, Alvin had spent too much time behind a desk, growing progressively rounder and less like the agents he led. Or he himself had been.

But now, the stress was showing. The man's hair was thinning appreciably and coming in all white. He had dropped weight, but that was due to not eating, rather than exercising more, so he moved stiffly, rather than the long, determined strides Royston had in his memory.

"Good morning, Sector Marshal," Royston smiled and tried to put a brave face on things. He was happy Pippa wasn't here to see how gray the man had turned in the last little bit.

"Hello, Royston," the man replied with a bit of a rasp to his voice as he walked over and shook hands. "I understand you have a new gadget for me, but that I needed to come down here to see it in private?"

"Indeed, old friend," Royston said. "This must remain at the highest security level for the time being."

Royston picked up the smaller device and handed it to the Sector Marshal.

"This is for you, to carry with you at all times," Royston's voice turned serious. "It will detect a new portal opening and sound an noise similar in volume to a breech alarm, which should awaken you and anyone close by that they are in danger."

"Thank you," Alvin took it and slid the device into his pants pocket. "And the other?"

"The other is a more powerful version, with a greater detection range," Royston said. "It will also project a small hologram showing you a vector to a portal it detects, with a reasonable range, but it not enough to cover the entire base."

"Should we build more?" Siddall asked. "Cover both this base and Headquarters with them? Perhaps the Hall of Governments down in Zurich, as well?"

"Perhaps, my friend," Royston said. "But if you do, it must be done quietly. Most people are not aware of the ability to open portals, and if such knowledge gets out, we will have other problems."

"Crime, yes," Alvin said. "It is driving me crazy, trying to find a way to prevent some Lawless Joe from just stepping into a bank vault and making off with all the gold. Or worse, pushing a bomb through and committing acts of terrorism."

"Just so," Royston said. "I can't prevent them. Not today. But I can know now that something happened, if it becomes necessary to solve a crime. So we must not let the lesser angels know of the solar system know of such a machine."

"What about the aliens?" Alvin's voice fell to a hoarse whisper. "Can we stop them?"

"We cannot." Royston was apologetic. "And I have no way of reaching out to them to even find out if they are helping us or setting us up for some grand invasion later."

"Welcome to my nightmares, Royston, old chap," Alvin said.

"I have a few ideas, Alvin," Royston said. "I plan on taking a week or three off shortly so that I can pursue them in a non-academic setting."

"What does that even mean?" the Sector Marshal's brow furrowed.

"Rock and roll, of all things, provided me the inspiration last time, Siddall," Royston grinned. "Teenage rebellion. I'm hoping something like it can show me the way to deflect portals, or prevent them entirely over a volume."

"I might sleep again, if you did," the big man grinned back. "Consider your vacation request approved in advance. And anything else you might need along the way."

"Thank you," Royston said, picking up the second machine and handing it to the Sector Marshal. "Put this in the station's Command Chamber and instruct them to contact you or I, or even Pippa, if it goes off, and then wait for orders."

"Your daughter?" Alvin scowled, mildly offended by his tones.

"My intellectual partner, Alvin," Royston fired back. "She is more knowledgeable about all of this than anyone else, including Sir West. And she had a good head on her shoulders in an emergency. I truly wish Earth Force would get over their male supremacy tendencies and realize that they are leaving out half the population as useful, contributing scientists."

"That is out of my hands, Royston," he said. "But

I will set this up and leave those orders. And perhaps that will help others see past the Women's Auxiliary Uniform to the mind and heart underneath."

He nodded and turned the go, pausing suddenly and pivoting back.

"Oh, dear," The Sector Marshal said. "I had forgotten. You have a visitor that that arrived on station late yesterday. We've been clearing her paperwork and following up. She's Persian, so we don't have a lot of background or context, but she's apparently a niece of your old nemesis, Firuz Alinejad."

They both smiled at the reference.

"Firuz was hardly a nemesis, Alvin," Royston laughed. "Except perhaps during the World Cup. The world lost a great mind when he died in that accident."

"Just so," Alvin nodded. "But his niece apparently inherited his brains and is a member of the Women's Auxiliary, in the same sort of situation as Pippa. Basic degree and nowhere to study the advanced stuff to challenge what the files say is a first-rate mind. Someone in our Persian office approved her to come here, with an eye to studying."

"Why is she here?" Royston asked.

"You apparently have a soft spot for letting women learn, Royston," Alvin laughed and headed for the door. "She checks out, but I wanted to prep you, rather than just letting her walk in an introduce herself to you."

"Thank you, old friend," Royston said as the door opened and the Sector Marshal departed.

Firuz Alinejad's niece? All well and good.

Except that he remembered getting half-drunk

with the man as they watched a World Cup final more than a decade ago, listening to him kvetch that nobody in his family had the brains Allah gave a goose.

So who was this woman?

# NIGHTFALL

NORMALLY, Gareth knew, it would have required a bit of work to track down all references to all the Gonquahs in the system. Especially as Gonquah belonged to a culture that didn't do last names, but just usually combined two or three syllables as a first name and called good. Or rather, all of the Th'Tarni used the exact same last name, which was the same thing, so *Accord* systems didn't even bother with them.

At the same time, the Constabulary had been gunning for the Th'Tarni merchant for years, however secretly and unsuccessfully, so getting Gareth everything known about the man and his business had only taken them a few days. That included the rough layouts of the factory Gareth wanted to break into, as they had to be kept up to date with the local fire suppression forces.

So he knew where he was going, and what he would see when he got there. He hoped.

The night was dark and warm. A little overcast, as

if perhaps it might make up its mind to throw howling thunderstorms later, but it was still just pregnant with heat and potential at this point.

That worked to their benefit. Gareth and Constable Baker were a few kilometers away, and more than a kilometer in the air, watching.

Gareth had never flown a lifterpack before, but it made perfect sense, once the mechanic had explained it to him and fitted him for the device. Small anti-gravity lifters neutralized your weight until you were effectively buoyant. Internal induction fans with vectored thrust nozzles could move you around like a hummingbird, or let you chase down a hawk if you needed to.

Baker was watching through a set of helmet optics that included magnification and light amplification. They were talking on a low-powered radio so they could be extremely quiet, even if they stumbled into the guards walking the facility.

"You ready?" she asked, flipping the scanner faceplate up into her helmet so he could see her eyes.

"Yes, ma'am," Gareth replied, pitching himself forward and pushing the button to accelerate his fans. This was almost as much fun as free-swimming in an orbital facility, a skill all Sky Patrol agents had to master.

She was a beat behind him, but slid onto his flank like a wingman flying a patrol in a fighter jet. Below them, the city stretched out, quiet like it was already anticipating trouble later.

Gareth told himself he was just being paranoid, but at the same time, Gonquah was also someone who dealt with Marc Sarzynski, so he wasn't sure it was possible to be too paranoid. Just in case, he had a stun pistol on his right thigh and a heavy disintegrator on his left.

The latter was a weapon capable of destroying an auto-taxi, but Gareth had no idea what the capabilities of a killer robot might be. He also figured that he wouldn't be liable for damages if the man was selling them to Maximus.

And Gareth still had the slightest juvenile delinquency streak, if he was being honest with himself. A standard disintegrator might do the trick, but the heavy version would be so much more entertaining if push came to shove.

They approached the building slowly. It was several stories high, but most of that was just vaulted space with catwalks connecting various manufacturing lines and machine systems. The roof itself was only slightly pitched from a central keel, and made of metal, so Gareth presumed landing on it would still make a noise like a drum.

With that in mind, the plan was for them to land in a quiet corner and force open a door, hopefully by picking the lock, but he could still annihilate it if he had to. They had the warrants duly signed and executed, so it wasn't criminal destruction. He just wanted to sneak up on that bastard if he could.

The outside was mostly dark on this side of the building. A loading dock was mildly busy on the other side, filling and emptying trucks at night, when most of the employees would be off, so they wouldn't be in the way.

Gareth and Baker just had to stay away from the few people moving around. Unless he wanted to arrest everyone and unscramble it all later. There was always that.

He suspected Baker was actually looking forward to that sort of thing. She could be like that.

They landed in a back yard with grass and tables. The map had it marked as a break area for employees, but the folks on the docks had their own, several hundred meters away around a corner, so hopefully they didn't need to walk clear over there for peace and quiet.

It was dark enough here.

"Should we leave the lifters?" he asked.

That had been the original plan, but she was in charge.

"Yes," Baker decided. "They are too obvious if someone sees us, while from a distance we might just be two employees walking along."

Gareth stripped quickly out of the oversized backpack, leaving only a set of black clothes built by Talyarkinash for covert missions. Baker did the same, drawing a set of compact tools from a pocket as they approached the door. Gareth drew the stunner for now and shifted to one side to keep watch behind them.

He had never picked a mechanical lock before. The theory itself was relatively simple, but it took a lot of practice to do it without breaking the lock or leaving a trace that you had passed through.

In his time, Gareth had always knocked politely. Or kicked the door in with beams blazing. But he could learn.

Eveth had it open almost as fast as Gareth suspected he might be able to get it with the key in one hand, but he didn't ask how. She was a cop. And a damned good one.

She passed through first, with him a step behind.

Inside, they were in a space that reminded him of an enlisted man's wardroom, with a number of tables where people could eat their lunch without having to leave the building. From which they could then step outside and have some sun. Or a smoke. Or something.

They crossed the space quickly and emerged into what Gareth thought of as storage. That spot where you put things you didn't need immediately on hand, out of the way of the folks on the floor, and not taking up precious loading dock space.

It made a useful spot to sort of hide in while they studied the interior. Gareth was reminded of a factory for making automobiles, with large overhead cranes that would carry a big piece along as teams did things to it, before you attached the wheels at the end and it could roll on its own.

He followed Baker from there to a stairway that got them up onto one of the catwalks. They were more exposed up here, but had a much better view in all directions. The lights were turned way down over most of the facility, so they should be okay as long as they moved slowly and stuck to shadows.

Carefully, they crept forward, staying out of sight as much as possible.

"And I'm telling you that somebody in your department signed for it two days ago," an angry voice suddenly echoed up from right beneath them.

Gareth froze, his stunner pointed down as two men walked exactly beneath he and Baker. She had drawn her own pistol and remained utterly still watching.

"And I wasn't here two days ago, so I got no clue what the hell you're talking about pal," the other man answered angrily. "Ask him where he put it."

"He's not here, so I gotta ask you," the first man yelled. "Maybe if your people weren't all fuckups we wouldn't have this problem. You ever imagine that?"

The angry noises faded as the two men turned a corner, but Gareth suspected that they would be going at it for a while. Or things would get out of hand and somebody would throw a punch.

That would actually work in his favor, as a fight back over there would draw more people from the inside of the factory and give he and Baker space to work.

As long as nobody walked out that rear door and saw a pair of lifterpacks stashed against the side of the building. Then the gig would be up.

They moved again quickly, just in case the men came back. To the end of the current run and sideways, it got them over a massive machine that Gareth thought might be a welding robot. It really didn't matter, as long as it got them out of sight.

Baker stopped so suddenly that Gareth nearly walked into her back.

"I had my doubts," she said as she quickly knelt down, using a handy I-beam pillar as cover.

Gareth studied her eyes and turned to see what had gotten her attention.

Robots. Two of them. Just exactly the sort of things he would have built, had he been commissioned to build *Androids*.

They stood watch on either side of a closed door to a section of the factory sealed off from the rest.

Each of them carried a disintegrator pistol in its right hand. Gareth would have expected Gonquah to arm them with stunners, but you apparently had to cross some level of security to get as far as that door, so anybody reaching those robots knew what they would find.

Or were up to no good and needed to be stopped.

Gareth had found what he had suspected from Gonquah's stories.

Now, he had to find the rest of the story.

# ANDROID

SHE HAD HAD HER DOUBTS. However, even Eveth Baker was willing to admit she had been wrong. She kept thinking of humans in terms of Gareth Dankworth, but that man was a born cop who lived and breathed doing the right thing. While his suggestions weren't always the legal thing, he was possessed of an innate ethical standard that had challenged even her from time to time.

Marc Sarzynski, on the other hand, was the death of all civilization boiled down and decanted into the form of a Vanir devil. A killer with absolutely no remorse, willing to say or do literally anything that would bring him closer to ultimate power.

Now, was one of those times when she wondered how bad things would have already gotten if those two idiot Yuudixtl hadn't had a change of heart and tried to stop the human on their own. Not that she would have believed them, if they had just walked into a Constabulary Station and turned themselves in. And that assumed that they had found honest cops.

Eveth was simultaneously appalled and outraged at how many bent cops had been discovered over the last few months as her and Grodray's investigations caused organizations to unravel and paperwork listing crimes and bribes to be revealed.

But this, this was something entirely else. There was no word for it in the *Accord*, so they had been forced to adopt a human word, like so many other situations.

Warfare. The systematic, industrialized killing of organic creatures, most of whom would be innocents caught in the middle. For that, Eveth could see the ultimate sanction being applied. She would make that case with Grodray and whoever else might listen, all the way up to the First Inspector, if necessary.

Two of Gareth's *androids* guarded a door. She and Gareth were wearing their Constabulary bodysuits, with black, civilian jackets thrown over that to make them look less like cops at a distance.

If someone got that close, it would already be time to either start shooting or call in Grodray with the Heavy Rescue Team he had on tap a few kilometers away. Gareth didn't know, because…

She wasn't sure why Grodray hadn't decided to tell Gareth. Maybe to inspire the man to be even more self-sufficient? Gareth was willing to go in alone already, so her quietly bringing up some heavy artillery wouldn't have changed anything.

And Gareth could be trusted. Nothing the man had ever done suggested otherwise. She made a mental note to ask Jack later. It hadn't seemed important then, but neither of them expected this, either.

The whole universe had just changed, if people like Gonquah were willing to supply people like Maximus with killer robots.

She measured the distance to the machines, but her disintegrator might not do the trick from here. Gareth's would, but they would still have a major distance to cover, even if he managed to destroy both machines.

"Back up," she ordered. "We'll circle around."

The big Vanir nodded and moved like a jungle cat, so utterly silent and fluid that Eveth felt a twinge of jealousy. And she was among the best.

But she knew what Dr. Liamssen had done to the human. Frighteningly, she also knew how much more capacity the form had, if they chose to go further at a later date.

Would the Chaa be offended if a new god was born in their ancient home? Eveth had never been a religious type. She knew the old stories handed down, and didn't doubt them, given all the other species that made up the *Accord*, but were people like Liamssen playing with fire now?

How far would be too far?

They moved. Back up the catwalk and to a space dark enough she felt comfortable descending to the factory floor. It was cooler down there, cold concrete underfoot acting as a heat sink and all the warm air rising up to the catwalk.

She kept two walls of equipment she couldn't identify between her and the machines on her right, and the loading dock on her left, tracking both locations on a detailed mental map as she moved.

Gareth remained three steps behind her and to the right, but she still had to glance back occasionally to make sure he hadn't vanished.

Utter silence, from one of the biggest Vanir she had ever known.

There was no way to know how good the sensors on the machines were, short of opening one up in a shop or locating the design specs that had been supplied, so Eveth had to guess when she would be close enough to hurt those machines, but not so close that she triggered a response from them first.

Fortunately, she was an even better shot than Gareth was.

This was probably close enough. At least she hoped.

"Just around this corner, at an angle of approximately forty degrees," she whispered up to Gareth. "I will shoot the one on the left. You shoot the one on the right. Then we'll get through that door and see what's inside. Questions?"

"Negative, sir," Gareth said.

It sounded automatic, rather than insulting. Gareth returning to an younger version of himself, fresh out of whatever the Earth Force Sky Patrol equivalent of Constabulary School was. Snapping to.

Eveth checked her pistol one more time. Charged. Safeties both off. Beam setting standard, rather than the short-range focus you might use to open an armored door or a safe. She noted Gareth doing the same and felt a surge of power go through her.

She had never tried to storm a building with Grodray, but she suspected that the man was hiding extreme competence in that field as well under that phlegmatic exterior. Gareth Dankworth was a Vanir of action, who had done this sort of thing before numerous times. She wouldn't have to worry about him freezing up.

Eveth took a breath and shifted just a little to her left. Not enough to be seen, but it gave Gareth a touch of space, since he would be a step behind her.

"Go," she said quietly.

Eveth stepped around the corner at a normal pace, but immediately knew she had misjudged the machines. Or their orders.

A pair of disintegrator pistols started to rise, so she snapped off a shot at her target. It was hurried and a little low, but good enough, even at thirty meters. She caught the machine in the right leg. Its knee exploded in a flash of sparks and superheated metal, knocking its torso forward and off-line.

That was good, because a wooden crate not far in front of Eveth exploded when the robot's own pistol fired.

She snapped off a second shot as fast as the weapon would cycle, aware that the android was doing the same thing. This one went center mass, but the machine was on its face on the concrete floor, so the head exploded, scalloping a divot out of the chest that shot sparks for several seconds.

Beside her, Gareth's heavier beam had struck his target center and a little high, ripping the top half of the torso away from the bottom and scattering metal parts everywhere.

It hadn't sounded all that much like thunder and lightning, but she hoped that whoever might have heard it in the building had presumed that the storm outside was either moving closer or had finally broken.

As she moved forward at a hard jog, it dawned on Eveth that Gareth was so much faster than she was that he had taken an extra step forward and still gotten a kill shot on his first try. She suspected that anyone other than her might be subject to an inferiority complex, knowing what Gareth could do, but Eveth also knew that she was still close to the top one hundred of her kind, across however many millions of Vanir there might be in the galaxy.

She could live in a world where Gareth was in the top three, as long as she could remove Maximus from the running. Preferably personally, given the opportunity.

Gareth arrived first, pulling the disintegrator pistol from the dead robot before removing the power pack and stuffing it into a pocket. She did the same as Gareth lifted the first machine and slid it behind some nearby crates, where it was more or less out of sight for now.

Eveth drew her stun pistol in her off hand and kept watch while he moved the second robot. She was ambidextrous with pistols, but having a stunner in her off hand meant that she had options.

If she wanted.

"Do we kick the door in, or pick the lock?" Gareth asked quietly as he stepped close.

"Is it locked?" she asked, watching his face fall and turn red in embarrassment.

He was a good cop, but still a little too linear.

Instead of answering, he grabbed the handle in his left hand, the one without the heavy disintegrator that had done such a good job on the first machine, and turned the knob.

"Me first," Eveth said, stepping forward.

Gareth pressed the door in just enough to clear the jamb, and then stepped back.

Eveth put her shoulder into the reinforced metal and pushed slowly.

Now, they would see what the hell Gonquah was really up to.

PENETRATION AGENT

THE ELEVATOR RIDE WAS QUICK, and then there would be a good deal of walking and riding on a sliding sidewalk to get there. Fatima took the time to be something of a tourist, understanding that no one from the *Accord* had ever actually been aboard this facility before. Just visiting Earth itself had been enough of a risk for the few anthropologists who had done it over the last few centuries. Now they were reaching that perilous stage where anything might be possible. Or necessary.

Including xenocide.

Fatima hoped that it was a good sign that the Sector Marshal himself, a human named Alvin Siddall, had come to escort her to the laboratory of her target, Dr. Royston Loughty, PhD, WMU, FRS, CBE, CStJ. Doctor of Physics as a Stellar Radiation expert. Warden of the Mathematical Union, apparently representing advanced, human scholars of mathematics. Fellow of the Royal Society, an insular, British organization of scientists dating back to the pre-Industrial Age. Commander, British Empire, and Commander, Order of St. John, representing prestigious awards for service to the British Throne, itself on a small island located off the northwest coast of the tiny peninsula called Europe, from which so much recent human history, for both good and ill, had originated.

Loughty was going to be a formidable opponent, of that she had no doubts. On the simple basis of the two Yuudixtl criminals kidnapping the Star Dragon, Gareth Dankworth, Loughty had come to envision and then articulate a higher level of physics than his culture should have been able to even imagine existed.

Worse, he had successfully translated that understanding into the very first wormhole generator in human history, a machine that would eventually allow them to access the entire galaxy, including invading the *Accord of Souls*, once they found out that they were truly not alone among the stars.

Fermi had been right to question things, according to her recent studies of human science. And she could fill in a very good set of approximations for Drake, if the folks around here wanted to run the numbers on his formula and extrapolate out to the rest of this massive galaxy. And all the other ones in the neighborhood.

Thankfully, there weren't many advanced civilizations out there. Some had already come and gone over the last billion years, either *Ascending* to a higher form of existence like the Chaa, or managing to wipe themselves out entirely by luck, anger, or technology run amok. Most of the rest were simple and primitive, as humans had been fifty thousand years ago when the Chaa uplifted the *Accord*, by means of taking semi-intelligent animals that represented the peak of mental development on *Orgoth Vortai*, and turning them into the *Children of the Accord*.

And the Chaa had specifically excluded humans, but even then the species was intelligent and tool-using. Philosophers had argued for millennia as to the *why* of that decision, with no better understanding now than they had had then. Hopefully, she would never find out why it had occurred, because there was only one way to get the truth, and that would be from the very beings that had made that decision, fifty thousand years ago.

So she followed the Sector Marshal. He was an older human, as she understood the physical signs of aging from her crash course on them. He did not appear to be all that healthy, if she was interpreting things correctly, but had apparently known Dr. Loughty for decades, as well as having known the man whose niece she was impersonating, the real Fatima Darzi, a rotund housewife who had served in the Women's Auxiliary for several years before meeting a salesman and marrying him. They were happily living on a farm several hours north of Tehran, far from most modern civilization.

Fatima had never met the real woman, but studied her, and more importantly, their uncle, Firuz, enough to talk with the Sector Marshal. It helped that Uncle Firuz had been killed in a tragic automobile accident while still rather young. That gave her an opening that she could exploit, once the right computer records had been doctored to show an entirely different career path for one Fatima Darzi than had been the actuality. Being Persian, there were few people around who might be able to gainsay those records in person.

"So not really much of a football fan?" the Sector Marshal asked, apparently trying to make pleasant conversation as they rode.

"Afraid not, sir," she replied. "I was always too busy studying, frequently in secret while my football-starved family was concentrating on the day's match."

It even sounded reasonable.

Fatima had never watched the so-called World Cup, but did understand the sport humans called *football*. The *Accord* had a similar sport, usually separated down species lines at the professional level, as the Vanir had such a tremendous physical advantage over their neighbors.

"Shame," the human said. "We used to have tremendously fun parties watching the tournament. Your uncle and Royston would make outrageous bets on matches that were more practical jokes on one another than anything."

"So I've heard," Fatima offered as a deflection.

She could smile at the human and let him ramble. Apparently a match eleven years ago had been one of the highest scoring finales in Cup history, and everyone still talked about it like it happened yesterday. Fatima could enjoy the conversation. Football was a team sport, rather than an individual thing. And it did serve to rally large groups of humans into something less violent than war, even if those sorts of things were frequently seen as a substitute.

Anything that made humanity less violent, as they developed, should be supported, however outrageous it might be. She had even wondered if geneticists back home could come up with some chemical or organism they could introduce into Earth's various biospheres, that might render humans less violent and dangerous.

Knowing their luck, it would end up killing most of the population instead and turn the rest into cannibals, another human term with absolutely no equivalent in the *Accord*.

Maybe wiping them all out really would be the only option.

"Here we go," the human said as the slidewalk reached a break point.

Fatima watched carefully as the human disembarked, ready to catch the man if he stumbled, but he was apparently stable enough on his feet to make the transition. They moved to one side as others followed from behind them, and then went up a side corridor into a secured area.

Both of their badges worked to open a door into what smelled, even to Fatima's reduced senses, like a scientific facility. Exotic chemicals signals were strong enough she could pick them up with just her nose, rather than her tentacles, layered over with the kind of heavy ammonia smell she associated with destroying organic experiments that had gone awry.

Still the best way to clean a petri dish. Unless you wanted to expose it to deep space and then have to scrape the freeze-dried gunk off afterwards.

A second door opened to a third and then a fourth. Fatima found herself in a mechanical laboratory. The sort of place where a scientist could play with physical toys to extrapolate from mathematics and physics, as a way of perhaps building better gadgets.

Probably weapons, knowing humans, but sometimes a better dishwasher might come out of it as well.

The smells were greatly reduced here. The most prominent was a rich, sweet smell she could not identify for a second, before something in her brain registered tobacco smoke from her studies.

Dr. Loughty frequently carried a device called a pipe, wherein he burned the dried leaves of a particular type of plant that had been soaked in a variety of chemicals to give it a specific taste. Fatima didn't smoke, and didn't know anyone who did, but was aware that it happened.

"Where the Devil are you?" the Sector Marshal called out. "My secretary said you were around."

"In here, Alvin," a voice called back.

It was richer in tone than the Sector Marshal's. Deeper and more authoritative, but also friendlier. Presumably Dr. Royston Loughty.

Her target.

"This way, my dear," the man said, leading her around the big work bench and to another door that was open.

Inside, an older human male. Not quite as tall as the Sector Marshal, but in much better health, by comparison. Perhaps the same age, from the color of hair and lines on the face. Late-middle-age, she would have guessed, but this man was well-preserved, even as the Sector Marshal felt used up.

The human rose and smiled at her. He was dressed in English Tweeds, as she had expected from her studies, right down to the leather elbow patches on both arms. A clean, wooden desk separated them.

A second human rose as Fatima came into view. Female. Beautiful for any species. Much younger than the scientist, perhaps Fatima's apparent age, or just a few years older. She also wore the crimson and gold of the Women's Auxiliary, and was taller than Fatima.

She had very light skin, compared to the duskiness of Fatima's Grace heritage. Shoulder-length red hair and a freckles suggested a Scottish background, so this must be Philippa Adeline Loughty. *Pippa*. Daughter of Royston and Elizabeth. Intended fiancé of Gareth Dankworth, in other circumstances.

"Royston, it is my inestimable pleasure to introduce to you Ms. Fatima Darzi of the Women's Auxiliary," the Sector Marshal's voice took on new strength as he spoke. "Ms. Darzi, Dr. Royston Loughty and his daughter, Pippa."

Fatima shook hands with both in the human style, a thing apparently invented to show that you did not have a weapon in your hands as you approached a stranger.

"I will leave you in extremely good hands," the Sector Marshal said with a quick bow. "Hopefully, you will have a most pleasant stay with us and make great contributions to both Earth Force and Sky Patrol in your future."

He departed with a grin. Pippa closed the door

and Fatima found herself finally alone, sitting politely with two of the most dangerous humans alive.

She took a deep breath and prepared for the conversation of her lifetime.

MONSTERS

IF HE HAD BEEN ALONE, Gareth would have raged
fit for the gods themselves, but that wasn't an option
here. Eveth Baker didn't need to see him angry
enough to chew nails. To break things with his bare
hands.

She needed to know he was capable of restraint in
the face of this kind of adversity. That the Star
Dragon was a tool he could call upon, rather than an
example of the deep anger churning in his soul at
what Marc was trying to do.

Even Earth had moved past the phase of using
killer robots to solve their problems. The whole
existence of Earth Force was dedicated to never
letting things get that bad again. That Marc Sarzynski
had gone there showed just how far he had fallen
from the man Gareth had once been proud to call a
friend.

It wasn't going to be enough to merely stop the
criminal warlord Maximus. Dragging the carcass of
the android off and hiding it brought home to Gareth

that perhaps he really did need to destroy the man who had been his best friend. Bury him under the jail, as the old saying went, rather than ever letting him see the light of day again.

Gareth suppressed an angry sigh and made it a point not to grind his teeth. Eveth Baker needed him calm, rational, and effective.

Burning this entire facility to the ground and then salting the earth would have to wait for another day. And probably a calmer Constable. He could trust her and Grodray to see it done right tomorrow.

"Do we kick the door in, or pick the lock?" Gareth asked in a low, ambiguous tone, trying not to let his emotions color the situation. The heavy disintegrator would probably do an awesome job of demolition.

"Is it locked?" Baker replied with a quick glance up.

Damn, he hadn't even considered that option. How far off true was he, right now?

Gareth grabbed the handle in his left hand and turned just enough to confirm that Baker was right. Not even locked. Just guarded by killer robots.

"Me first," she said, stepping into him from the side before he could move.

She would have hipchecked him out of the way, too. Well, at least tried. He still outweighed her by eight stone, give or take, but he gave way anyway, pushing the door in just enough to clear the jamb, and slowly letting go of the handle.

He watched her ease into a dark space, then stepped after her.

Gareth found himself in a hallway with two doors on either side. They felt like offices.

Past that was a wide opening that felt more like a

storage garage than a factory. Low ceilings and wide walls beyond created something like the hall where he had once gone to see a bunch of antique automobiles from the petroleum era and early electric period. The floor had a black and white parquet checkboard set into it, but most of the near space was clear.

Deeper back, the hall fell to darkness, but he could see light reflecting off metal back there. Hopefully nothing bad.

Baker led them to the first door on the right. It was an office space, generic and sterile. No pictures on the desk or backboard. Mass produced copies of water colors on two walls. Just a chair, a working surface, and a telephone, like a traveling manager would use this space when he was here, but would share it with a number of others.

She grunted, but made no other comment, so Gareth concentrated on calming thoughts, rather than setting fire to the desk and watching the flames lick walls hungrily. Now was most definitely not the time.

Across the hall, another office. This one looked lived in, with flowers and a picture of a Nari family: Mom, Dad, and two kits; on the backboard. The desk was locked, but Baker didn't try forcing any of the drawers.

Gareth figured that she could probably just rip the first drawer open, if she wanted to, then trip the switch to open the rest, but she could also get out her picks.

Maybe later, once they knew what was about.

The third door was another generic office. Unlived in and almost abandoned feeling.

The fourth space was the jackpot, as far as Gareth was concerned. A big table dominated the space, with several four-drawer file cabinets along the rear wall.

Someone had been working in here, and had not bothered to clean up when they left for the day. There was an android head resting on the table top like a victim of Dr. Guillotine's device. Around it, a number of blueprints, actually printed on off-white paper in blue ink, like back home, rather than just electronic files to be transmitted from machine to machine wirelessly.

Gareth studied the blueprint while Baker lifted the head and studied it. After a moment, his unconscious fascination with the document became clear. On the one hand, it did remind him of home, and did so in a good way, taking him back to the days of his first drafting class, when you had to start at the very beginning, with paper and pen, and only later learned how to use modeling software in your second semester.

On the other hand, it also looked familiar because he recognized the handwriting. How many years had they spent checking each other's homework to make sure they hadn't missed anything? He missed that guy, too, but they were long past those days, and would never get them back.

He was holding the proof in his hands, signed **MS** in the bottom right, just like the old days.

*Marc Sarzynski, Destroyer of Worlds.*

Gareth tore off the top page and folded it up enough to stuff into a pocket on his belt. If nothing else, that one piece of paper was all the evidence he needed to shut this place down and have Gonquah hauled away, even if killer robots with disintegrators guarding the front door somehow bizarrely failed to meet a standard necessary for a grand jury to indict.

Now, he had the connection he needed back to Maximus. He could burn this place down. Or rather, have it seized. Gareth let go of his anger long enough to consider all the men and women who would be out of work tomorrow if he destroyed this factory, much as he wanted to.

He let the heat simmer, since there was no way to turn it off.

"You okay?" Baker was suddenly standing next to him, concern etched on her face.

"Angry," he replied, figuring that honesty was the best choice here. "But we've got them both."

He pointed to the remaining stack of papers, tapping the MS signature on each one. And Gareth would be happy to testify as a handwriting expert personally familiar with Sarzynski's scrawl.

He doubted that he would ever be able to take the man alive, though. He would still try. That was who he was.

"MS," Baker said. "Marc Sarzynski?"

"That's his handwriting," Gareth murmured. "Know it as well as my own."

She tapped the page and studied it.

"Simple enough," she said, tracing lines and pistons. "Amazing that it could be so dangerous."

"The programming for safe robots back home is the product of thousands of man-months of work," Gareth noted. "Here, you just skip all that and aim the damned thing. Do we have enough to call in the Constabulary and turn this place over?"

"Let's see what's in the space beyond this," Baker

said. "But yes, this will be enough to blow up in Gonquah's face and let us sweat him. Hopefully, he'd rather give up Sarzynski than take all the heat himself, but this will be more than he can wriggle out of, this time."

Gareth nodded and kept his opinions to himself. Death by fire breath was not the solution right now. He was a cop, not a rogue elephant.

By the book. By the law. By the standards of justice.

Not just revenge. Much as he was seeing red right now.

Tomorrow, hopefully, he could start hunting his old friend.

And kill the man.

Baker watched him like she could see the internal monologue. Maybe she could. Gareth wasn't trying to hide anything right now. Just control it and get the damned job done.

"Let's go," she finally said, when she had decided that he was under control.

He nodded and followed her back out into the hallway.

Right, and they entered that big arcade. It was dark in here, with just the standard emergency exit lights and a few others. Gareth was still absently holding the disintegrator in one hand, mostly as a security blanket rather than a threat, so he reached for a flashlight from his belt.

Baker turned and walked to the side of the doorway. She ran her hand up to flip several switches, and suddenly it was as bright as day in here.

Gareth apparently muttered the word out loud,

instead of just inside his head. That, or Baker was thinking the same thoughts, because she said the profanity much louder as she turned back to the room.

It was a showroom, of sorts. Fifty meters wide and at least one hundred and twenty deep, it was, mercifully, mostly empty. That was good, because Gareth guessed there were perhaps as many as a hundred more of the androids at the far end, lined up perfectly still, like troops awaiting an inspection.

Gareth found the scene drawing him closer. Baker came along in his wake, but neither of them spoke.

He was just thankful that these machines were not armed, like the two they had destroyed out front. One hundred was an entire company, going back to the days of organized armies. God only knew what someone could do with that sort of force here in the *Accord*.

Up close, they were even more frightening. All-steel bodies with protective knobs around the joints. Human sized, so they felt to Gareth like twelve-year-olds, but he could see how intimidating a six foot tall robot would be to Nari or Grace, who tended to be a shade smaller. And if he was designing them, and he knew the man who had, they would be at least as strong as a Vanir. Probably more, since Marc knew what Gareth had turned into.

Metal heads like motorcycle helmets. Eyes and mouth, with just a suggestion of a nose and simple holes for ears. At least Marc hadn't added antennae or something, like a Traakna had, and this model just had hands.

Gareth could imagine a dedicated model with a heavy blaster of some kind permanently attached to the forearm, or perhaps replacing it altogether as a walking anti-tank gun.

This all needed to be destroyed before it got loose into the *Accord*. They might never recover.

"That's it," Baker announced in a voice that even came close to approximating the rage in Gareth's breast. "I'm calling this in."

He watched her pull a comm from her belt, but suddenly the android closest to her turned his head and stared right at Baker.

"Intruder alert," the android said in a crude, mechanical voice.

It started to step forward, arms coming up to apparently grab Baker, and Gareth did the only thing he could think of.

He punched it across the jaw. Which was a stupid thing to do, since it was metal, and he was holding a heavy disintegrator in his other fist, but something had snapped in him.

And while he knocked down the first android, all of the rest of them began to move.

# END TIMES

EVETH HAD BEEN CONCERNED about how close to the edge Gareth seemed to be. Or rather, just how shallowly buried the man's intense anger was right now. But she was also impressed by the level of control he exhibited. That scored a lot of points in his favor, as far as she was concerned.

She would trust the man less if he was a true teenage Nature Scout, and not a grown adult with a full range of emotional potential. He was working to act like an adult, but she could almost smell the brimstone coming off of him, presumably at what Maximus had done, and might still do.

She could only imagine a hundred or more of these killer machines loose with beam weapons. Most cops only carried stunners because it was the easiest and safest way to stop a criminal from getting away, or if two people were fighting and wouldn't listen to commands.

That lit some of the same fire in her that apparently Gareth had been experiencing for the last few minutes, but he understood the implications in his soul, while she was only now truly wrapping her mind around the term "a threat to the entire *Accord of Souls*."

This wasn't academic. This was a conspiracy to overthrow everything and presumably institute a reign of terror as only humans could imagine and enforce.

"That's it," she said firmly, keeping her own emotions in check as Gareth had done. "I'm calling this in."

Eveth reached for her communicator as the android closest to her suddenly woke up and turned to look up at her.

"Intruder alert," the machine announced, reaching for her as she tried to back away.

Gareth surprised the hell out of her by punching the machine, and doing so hard enough to knock it over. But the others were moving. Waking up. Coming for her soul.

Eveth quick-drew her blaster and shot the closest one square in the chest before it even took its first step, but one hundred more were coming.

"Run," she ordered, turning and starting to move. Unless Sarzynski had programmed them to her sort of specs, she could make it to the door.

Behind her, two quick shots rang out, followed both times by the sort of sound you might get throwing a box of anvils down a staircase.

"Gareth," she yelled to get his attention. He seemed to be in a fog, backing away from the machine and shooting them, rather than fleeing. And she could see both wings starting to move forward and around the man. He would be encircled and possibly killed, depending on how these things reacted to intruders.

What would someone like Gonquah program into them, to keep his secrets safe?

Something about her voice broke through Gareth's attention.

"Baker," he yelled, acknowledging her and starting to come away from them. "Get help."

Yes, they were in trouble. The robots were moving faster now, as Gareth started to jog backwards. Like horsemen, they were about to flank him.

Eveth stopped and turned back.

"Mayday," she said into the comm. "Officers under fire. Require backup now."

Not entirely true, but that would get Jack and his team here the fastest. She fired a shot at the right side, winging a robot and knocking it down. A second shot grazed a closer one and hit one further away, damaging both but stopping neither.

Gareth was moving, but he had waited too long. That much was obvious. Hands began to clutch at him, even as he fired back over a shoulder and tried to run.

"Jack, this is Eve," she yelled into the comm. "Now, damn it."

More shots. Hers and Gareth's. It felt like trying to stop the tide from coming in with a shovel, but her partner was back there, and had been trying to protect her when they got in over their heads.

Gareth screamed in pain as one of the machines clipped his leg and he stumbled into another that grabbed on and held tight. Several more arrived and held.

She couldn't shoot into that melee without hurting Gareth, possibly killing him.

"Jack?" she yelled, suddenly afraid that they had gotten inside of a scrambler field as well, and nobody would ever come for her.

Eveth was about to abandon Gareth and run when her comm squelched.

"Inbound, Eve," Jack said in a hard, angry tone.

Gareth's anguished scream nearly stripped her soul raw, and then it changed, deepened. And it grew loud enough that anyone in the factory probably heard it. Or at least felt it in their own souls.

The Star Dragon. That was what the monster sounded like as it was reborn tonight.

Pure rage.

Eveth knelt and took a careful aim, blasting everything that moved close to Gareth. If she could get him free, maybe they had a chance.

The androids knocked Gareth down, and several more piled on top of him. For a moment, she wondered if they had been programmed to kill Gareth as their first priority, but a large group suddenly turned towards her and began to run. Faster than a Vanir could escape them.

Eveth gave up shooting and ran for her own life. Gareth had the Star Dragon. She only had whatever Jack could bring.

And however long it took that team to get here.

She reached the hallway, just as a flying android slammed face first into the wall beside her and went clear through into the office beyond.

She looked back, to see the Star Dragon in full form, rolling and swatting with arms, legs, and tail as he was beset by a plague of bipedal rats.

A gout of flames behind her suddenly lit the entire room brighter than noonday sun. "Gareth?" she yelled, slowing just a little.

"Run," he commanded. "He made them fireproof."

Or course, she thought. Wouldn't you, after seeing that thing being born?

She almost made it.

Got her hands onto that outside door when two of the robots grabbed her from behind.

Eveth managed to kill one of them, but the other got hold of her pistol and ripped it away from her hard enough that she might have broken bones in her hand.

Not that it would matter, if they were both about to die.

The Star Dragon screamed in a rage so loud, so primal that she nearly almost screamed back in reaction, the sound ripped from her very soul.

A scaled hand suddenly grabbed the machine holding her and squeezed.

Even over her pounding heart, Eveth could hear the sound of metal deforming under that assault. She could do the same to a soft drink can, and that's what it looked like.

"Go," the Wyrm ordered as he blocked others from getting into the hallway to come after her.

Simple math, she realized as she fled.

Without a gun, she couldn't do anything here to alter the outcome.

Except die. There was always that.

Gareth was going to sacrifice himself to keep her alive, dying in the process of destroying as many of these androids as he could.

Eveth suppressed the profanity and put her energy into her legs.

She kicked that outer door hard enough to bounce it off the far wall, barely slowing as she ran.

Outside, a mob of men was running towards her.

Eveth was just going to have to kill all of them before they could help the robots kill Gareth. Jack would be here soon enough to avenge them both.

"Get her to safety," the closest man yelled.

Eveth focused on the speaker, and realized that it was Grodray, wearing his own lifterpack, with a matched pair of heavy disintegrators in his hands.

One of the others caught her and shifted her out of the way of a dozen men and women with rifles and pistols as they charged back up the hallway.

"Are you hurt?" the medic asked.

That woman had her own heavy disintegrator in a cross-draw holster under her arm, but was doing medical things now.

"Broken hand," Eveth held it out. "The rest is bruising."

From behind her, screams of pain gave way to the thunderous roll of several weapons firing as fast as they could cycle. The medic pulled her to one side.

Eveth truly wondered if the fabled End Times was upon them, just from the sound, so loud that it was a physical thing.

It felt like eternity has passed, but silence suddenly broke out.

"Gareth?" Eveth said.

"You need to stay here, Constable," the medic said firmly, trying to see how badly she was hurt.

"That's my partner," Eveth growled. "Give me your pistol. I'm going in there."

The medic started to argue, subsided, and handed Eveth her pistol. She moved to follow Eveth in.

"Medic," Grodray yelled, so the woman started to run.

Eveth kept pace.

The inside of the space looked like how she always envisioned a true battle would, if the humans ever escaped into the *Accord*. There were pieces of broken android every direction she looked, including embedded in the roof. There was blood everywhere, as well. Lots of it.

Grodray was kneeling next to one of his troopers.

When Eveth got there, she realized it was Gareth.

He looked like hell, but he was still breathing. Both eyes were blackened. As was most of his face. Blood from a cut in his hair had covered much of his chest and was dripping onto the floor.

His hands looked like he had slammed them in door, and then used a hammer to finish the job, gnarled and bloodied.

"Lie still, damn it," Grodray yelled, trying to hold Gareth down. "We got them."

"Baker?" he cried so pitifully it nearly broke her heart.

"I'm here, Gareth," she yelled back, falling her knees across from Grodray.

That seemed to get through to him. His head turned towards her and the medic slid in and just hit him with a heavy-duty pain-killer. Gareth had to be blind from all the blood and swelling, but she saw him smile for just a moment, before he passed out.

"Eve?" Grodray stood and lifted her to her feet.

"We've got Gonquah, Jack," she said. "Evidence is in one of the offices back there. I want him nailed to a wall this time. I'd be dead right now, if it wasn't for Gareth. And he'd be dead without you."

"Understood, Eve," Grodray said. "I've already got another team kicking in the man's front door as soon as a message gets there.

"Good," she said. "He and Sarzynski have started a war with the entire Constabulary. I'm going to destroy that son of a bitch."

# FRAUD

AS A MATTER OF COURSE, Royston would never have met with a young, single woman in the privacy of his office. They would have gone to one of the coffee shops on the station, or some other public place where nobody might be free to whisper things that would damage such a woman's reputation, even with a fussy old duffer such as himself.

He had his memories of Elizabeth, and a most wonderful daughter, so he did not foresee himself ever marrying again. Not that he would ever say never, but…

Today's meeting needed to be as private as it possibly could be. He needed an unimpeachable witness as well, one that would be believed, regardless of the story that she might tell later.

Pippa would make sure you were listening.

The three of them were alone. The door was closed. Presumably the Sector Marshal was returning to the Command Chamber, where he would count this as a successful meeting.

At least until Royston told him otherwise.

Royston smiled to put Ms. Darzi at ease. Pippa smiled as well. After a moment, the stranger relaxed, more or less.

"I remember Firuz Alinejad quite well," he announced, savoring some of those deep-into-the-night discussions and arguments over tea, as well as all the louder hijinks around the World Cup.

Truly, he missed his old friend.

"He was a good man," Darzi replied. "Warm and brilliant at the same time, when that so rarely happens."

"Indeed," Royston smiled at the young woman. "So how may I be of service, madam?"

"There are rumors that you are studying higher mathematics," this stranger, this *imposter* said carefully. She nodded politely to Pippa. "As with your daughter, I was unable to pursue my studies, as many people were offended that a woman might take such a slot at the university, when it should go to a man. If possible, I had hoped that I might be able to study under you."

Royston noted Pippa's look of mild surprise, but she had never really met Firuz, except when he and Elizabeth had hosted the man for an Eid dinner, or some other things where he might be one of the only Muslims around. And she had been only a teenager when the man died.

Pippa would only know about Fatima Darzi what the records showed, and not the sorts of things that might have never made it to a computerized record, where someone with intent and capability might tamper with it.

Royston let the moment drag, perhaps a little too

long. Pippa turned to him, as if to silently reproach him for rudely not responding, even if to let her know he was thinking about the topic.

He was indeed thinking about it. Just not the way either of these two women probably expected.

At least whoever it was had respected him enough to not throw a floozy at him. He could deal with them playing to his vanity and intellect. It would be downright insulting to suggest that a honeypot might have worked.

He would thank them for that, perhaps, if he ever got the chance.

"Father?" Pippa finally asked, perhaps amazed at how rude he was being.

But then, he was being rude.

And it was about to get worse.

Royston smiled at Pippa. He smiled at Fatima Darzi, or whoever she really was.

Mildly, he pulled open the top drawer to his desk and pulled out the pistol he had put in there earlier, when Alvin had mentioned Firuz's niece.

He had met the young lady. Well, teenager then, twelve years ago when he and Firuz had secretly snuck down to Tehran to watch a football match at his sister's house: Yasmina Darzi, born Yasmina Alinejad. Fatima Darzi had been an angry teenager in those days, plotting how to escape her family and run away from the city she saw as being so decadent as to threaten the very future of Persian society.

Too intellectual, when Allah offered all the answers a woman needed, none of which included western mathematics, even if the Persians had actually been the fathers of so much of the learning that Western Europe had later stolen and claimed for themselves.

He knew the woman had later served a quick tour of duty, just enough to appease her family, but he also knew she would never leave the surface of the Earth again voluntarily.

Royston centered the pistol on this imposter's chest and flipped the safety off rather noisily.

He had a smile, even as both women registered the immense shock of his appallingly bad manners. Pulling a blaster pistol in conversation could be like that.

"I think we can dispense with the silly notion that you are Fatima Darzi," Royston said with a steely tone. "Why don't you tell me who you really are, young lady."

"Father?" Pippa spoke, but didn't twitch.

That was good. Any motion at all right now and he would pull the trigger, assuming self-defense at this point as he annihilated the woman across from him and a reasonable chunk of the chair and wall behind her.

Darzi appeared to appreciate that. She kept her hands down on the arms of her chair and her body encased in ice.

The moment stretched.

"Or I could just shoot you and turn your body over to Alvin to investigate," Royston offered. "Your choice."

"That would be…unwise, Dr. Loughty," she said in a slow, deliberate voice.

It was a different tone. Calmer. More centered. Like another woman was inhabiting the flesh than the one who walked in here.

Staring at your death from violent beam weapons was almost as good as a hanging to center the mind.

"Would it now?" Royston found his voice getting light, like a cat patting at a mouse. "Why is that?"

"I am not what I seem," Darzi said.

"Oh you seem to me to be an imposter and a spy," Royston said politely. "Why shouldn't I shoot you?"

"I would like to show you the truth, Dr. Loughty," she said carefully. "I had hoped that it wouldn't come to that, but you've obviously thought much deeper about the implications of things than my superiors considered. If you will allow me to remove my hijab, much will become clearer, but I need to extract a promise from you, from both of you, that you will keep my secret. I can negotiate in good faith, if you will as well."

Good faith? From a spy? It would have probably worked, but for things nobody but he and Fatima would know.

"And if not?" Royston pursued the thread.

"Part of my mission was scouting, Dr. Loughty," she said. "But the First Inspector tasked me with finding a way to prevent a greater catastrophe, if that was possible."

"And removing your hijab will uncover the truth?" Royston was doubtful, but she wasn't as panicked as an amateur would be.

"It will," Fatima replied.

Royston considered it, and shook his head.

"You will remain perfectly still," he ordered. "Pippa can remove the cloth. I would hate to find that you had secreted a weapon of some kind up there and were able to get to it."

"Agreed, Dr. Loughty," Fatima said, nodding

with her eyes and nothing else. "Ms. Loughty, the hijab is tucked in under the right side and pinned behind my ear. More or less."

"Father?" Pippa asked carefully. She was out of her depth here, but Royston had been his own kind of agent, back in his youth. Even Elizabeth hadn't known the full truth about some of the things he had done at Gareth's age.

"Go ahead, Pippa," he directed her, lowering his point of aim a bit to catch the imposter in the belly rather than the heart.

Pippa rose and slid out of her chair, never getting between him and his target. She moved carefully and deliberately next to Fatima and reached out with just her left hand, probing.

"What?" Pippa flinched, nearly causing him to kill Fatima, but something in the imposter's eyes held the shot off.

"It's okay," Fatima said, sharply but calmly. "You will understand shortly."

Pippa reached again and found the pin. She extracted it and stuck it into her own blouse to keep it out of the way. Then she grabbed the hijab and pulled it up and away carefully and deliberately.

Royston had thought he had steeled his soul for anything, including a bomb hidden up there.

The truth was so much worse.

"What?" Pippa said before she caught herself.

Fatima's eyes never left Royston's.

"Those are sensory tentacles," she explained carefully. "I have taken drugs to keep them from moving, and in the process nearly blinded myself to all normal sensory input. I understand that to a human, I would look like the medusa of your

Hellenic legend, but that is not the case. I have no teeth, merely more senses, currently mostly asleep."

"What are you?" Royston's voice had fallen to a hoarse whisper.

"I am a *Grace*, Dr. Loughty," Fatima said. "One of the member species of a galactic organization known as the *Accord of Souls*. I have been sent here to find out how much you know, and how close you are to becoming an existential threat to the *Accord*."

"Threat?" he asked, aghast at this turn of events.

"Humans are seen as the greatest menace in the galaxy, sirrah," she snapped tartly. "Some members of the *Accord* have voted to wipe the species out, but they were always previously overruled, on the simple basis that humanity was trapped in this solar system and thus could not reach us. That has now changed."

"Wipe us all out?" Pippa asked.

Fatima turned slowly to look up at her, no other bit of her moving, except for the sluggish, snake-like tentacles she had instead of *hair*.

"It could have been a bomb as easily as a spy, Ms. Loughty," Fatima said coldly. "Or a bioweapon. We are trying to prevent that, if possible."

"We?" Royston asked.

"The Constabulary, Dr. Loughty," she replied. "I'm given to understand that it serves much the same purpose in the *Accord of Souls* as Earth Force Sky Patrol does here."

"How would you know that?" he demanded sharply.

"Gareth Dankworth told us," she replied.

# READ MORE!

Be sure to read all of the Star Dragon books!

*Birth of the Star Dragon*
*Flight of the Star Dragon*
*Call of the Star Dragon*
*Shadow of the Star Dragon*
*Trial of the Star Dragon*

# ABOUT THE AUTHOR

Blaze Ward writes science fiction in the Alexandria Station universe (Jessica Keller, The Science Officer, The Story Road, etc.) as well as several other science fiction universes, such as Star Dragon, the Collective, and more. He also writes odd bits of high fantasy with swords and orcs. In addition, he is the Editor and Publisher of *Boundary Shock Quarterly Magazine*. You can find out more at his website www.blazeward.com, as well as Facebook, Goodreads, and other places.

Blaze's works are available as ebooks, paper, and audio, and can be found at a variety of online vendors. His newsletter comes out quarterly, and you can also follow his blog on his website. He really enjoys interacting with fans, and looks forward to any and all questions—even ones about his books!

**Never miss a release!**
If you'd like to be notified of new releases, sign up for my newsletter.

I will never spam you or use your email for nefarious purposes. You can also unsubscribe at any time.

http://www.blazeward.com/newsletter/

**Connect with Blaze!**

Web: www.blazeward.com
Boundary Shock Quarterly (BSQ):
https://www.boundaryshockquarterly.com/

f  facebook.com/KRPBlaze
g  goodreads.com/Blaze_Ward

# ABOUT KNOTTED ROAD PRESS

Knotted Road Press fiction specializes in dynamic writing set in mysterious, exotic locations.

Knotted Road Press non-fiction publishes autobiographies, business books, cookbooks, and how-to books with unique voices.

Knotted Road Press creates DRM-free ebooks as well as high-quality print books for readers around the world.

With authors in a variety of genres including literary, poetry, mystery, fantasy, and science fiction, Knotted Road Press has something for everyone.

Knotted Road Press
www.KnottedRoadPress.com